"I want you so bad…"

They were at the point of no return.

"Just like old times." A crooked, cocky smile crested Jayson's firm mouth. "That's what you said the last time we were in here about to do this for the first time."

"You remember that?"

"I remember everything, G." There was something tender about that statement. Too tender. It reminded her of how tender that first time was, and how in love they once were. Before life became about him corralling her energy and needing to be the Fixer of All Things.

"I don't have a condom," she said since that was the first unromantic comment that popped into her head.

"I do." He frowned. "In my room."

She shook her head. "We're not risking that again."

Gia was supposed to be in charge of her faculties—she was a certified genius, after all. But Jay weakened her knees…*still*.

***

One Last Kiss by Jessica Lemmon is part of the Kiss and Tell series.

Dear Reader,

I can't believe we've reached the end of the Kiss and Tell series already! Did that go as fast for you as it did for me?

To wrap up the Knox family saga, I'm giving Gia Knox-Cooper and Jayson Cooper a shot at redeeming themselves. A year and a half ago they divorced, believing that their separation was the end of them as a couple, but fate (and this author) has a different plan for them...

When an issue at work forces these ex-spouses to work together for a common goal, Jayson and Gia must face their past. The attraction is still alive and well, but what about the other issues that kept them from understanding each other? Can they finally close the gap, or will they stay in their separate corners and guard their hearts?

As with every romance I write for you, this one has a happy ending. But if you ask me, the fact that they lost each other and then find their way back to each other makes it that much sweeter.

Happy reading!

Jessica Lemmon

PS: Be sure to sign up for my newsletter for behind-the-scenes goodies, cover reveals and announcements for what's coming next at www.jessicalemmon.com.

JESSICA LEMMON

ONE LAST KISS

 **HARLEQUIN®**

DESIRE™

Recycling programs
for this product may
not exist in your area.

ISBN-13: 978-1-335-20922-1

One Last Kiss

Copyright © 2020 by Jessica Lemmon

This edition published by arrangement with Harlequin Books S.A.

For questions and comments about the quality of this book,
please contact us at CustomerService@Harlequin.com.

Harlequin Enterprises ULC
22 Adelaide St. West, 40th Floor
Toronto, Ontario M5H 4E3, Canada
www.Harlequin.com

Printed in U.S.A.

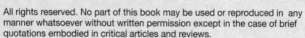

A former job-hopper, **Jessica Lemmon** resides in Ohio with her husband and rescue dog. She holds a degree in graphic design, which is currently gathering dust in an impressive frame. When she's not writing supersexy heroes, she can be found cooking, drawing, drinking coffee (okay, wine) and eating potato chips. She firmly believes God gifts us with talents for a purpose, and with His help, you can create the life you want.

Jessica is a social media junkie who loves to hear from readers. You can learn more at jessicalemmon.com.

Books by Jessica Lemmon

Harlequin Desire

Dallas Billionaires Club

Lone Star Lovers
A Snowbound Scandal
A Christmas Proposition

Kiss and Tell

His Forbidden Kiss
One Wild Kiss
One Last Kiss

Visit her Author Profile page at Harlequin.com, or jessicalemmon.com, for more titles.

You can also find Jessica Lemmon on Facebook, along with other Harlequin Desire authors, at Facebook.com/harlequindesireauthors!

For those of you who believe in second chances.

Prologue

Five and a half years ago, New Year's Eve

"Daddy," Gia Knox said from between clenched teeth. But her father, busy bragging on her as per his usual, wouldn't be dissuaded. His current brag was her graduating the Massachusetts Institute of Technology with honors, and the impressive work she would soon do at the family company, ThomKnox.

"She inherited her brains from me, of course." Jack Knox gave his only daughter a wink and wrapped an arm around her.

"Don't be silly, Jack," Gia's mother, Macy, interjected. "Everyone knows our daughter inherited her intelligence from me. Let's leave these kids alone. We're ruining their fun."

Macy whisked Jack away so suddenly, Gia was left alone with one of the most talented web designers in the company. She shuffled her feet as best she could in black Louboutins, clasping her hands in front of her black glittery skirt. By the time she was fiddling with her long beaded necklace over her sequined top, she realized she was having a rare awkward moment.

"Sorry about that," she muttered to the man before her. "They're proud. Anyway, it's great to meet you, Jayson."

"Cooper," he said, the deep timbre of his voice glancing off each one of her ribs. "No one calls me Jayson."

"Well, then I definitely won't call you Cooper. I pride myself in being unique." She'd meant the quip to be a cute conversation salve to the embarrassing display by her dad, but it came out sounding flirty. And Jayson responded.

"You, Gia Knox, are definitely unique." His smile twitched beneath a trimmed neat goatee before vanishing. That half smile was completely attractive. Disarmingly so. All of him was. He had broad shoulders and wore a suit well. She'd surreptitiously checked him out more than once while her father was rattling off her GPA.

Jayson's thick wavy dark hair was cut professionally and close, but his facial hair lent him an air of mystery. And those eyes. Blue and piercing, she'd bet they didn't miss a thing.

"Well, then, Jay," she said, testing the new nickname and receiving an eyebrow arch in response, "you'll either be enchanted or disappointed to hear I'm joining the tech team."

"Enchanted," he answered without hesitation. "Definitely enchanted."

"Sixty seconds!" Her brother Brannon called out, blowing into a noisemaker and earning a round of cheers and applause. Nearly every employee of Thom-Knox was present at the New Year's Eve celebration, including Gia's family since they *were* ThomKnox.

Partygoers followed Bran's lead and pressed in toward the center of the ballroom, leaving Jay and Gia to watch them go.

"The moment we've all been waiting for," she said as the crowd began a sloppy midnight countdown at the thirty-second mark. "A bunch of employees making out at the stroke of the new year."

This time when her gaze clashed with Jayson's, it stuck. She found herself unable to look away. The moment his eyes left hers they took an inventory of her mouth.

She felt the brush of his gaze the way she might have felt his hand. Or his lips. It was intimate. It was heady. He had her thoroughly distracted and totally off-kilter. She'd had one glass of champagne, no more, but felt as if she'd polished off a bottle and then someone had hit her over the head with it.

Had she ever met a guy and felt this much *longing*? And what was it about *him*—but she knew. Jayson was as charmed by her as she'd been by him. Rarely was attraction ever that equal.

At that second—and the three that followed—she imagined satisfying her longing and kissing Jayson

Cooper. Lifting to her toes and pressing her mouth to his. He smelled good from where she stood, and she'd bet he was absolutely intoxicating close up.

There's only one way to find out.

Jayson, his gaze trickling back up to hers, leaned forward the slightest bit.

Then a red-haired woman who was even shorter than Gia and wearing a skirt that was a lot tighter than Gia's, crashed into him.

"Cooper, come *on*! We'll miss the countdown!" The redhead bounced as she wrapped both her arms around one of his. Her headband bobbed, the words *Happy New Year* waving. "Hi," she chirped. "I'm Shelly."

"Gia Knox." Gia shook the other woman's hand, feeling the loss of Jayson's attention when he rigidly looped his arm around his date's waist.

As if summoned, Gia's boyfriend, Tom, approached. "There you are."

Tom leaned in to kiss her cheek and she pasted on a plastic smile.

"It was nice to meet you, Jay," Gia called as Tom pulled her toward the crowd. Jayson nodded, his frown slight but visible, as Shelly towed him to the middle of the room.

Gia and Jay watched each other as the countdown continued, as more and more distance separated them and more and more people came between them.

Three.

Two.

One.

"Happy New Year!" the crowd shouted as silver and gold confetti rained down on the ballroom.

"Happy New Year, baby," Tom said to Gia and then captured her mouth in a kiss. She pushed aside the inconvenient—and possibly insane—attraction she felt toward Jayson and focused on her date. But Tom's kiss barely registered on her *oh, baby* scale. Her heart wasn't racing the way it was a moment ago. Her stomach wasn't clenched in delicious anticipation as it had been a moment ago.

She leaned into the kiss, determined to bury that errant blip of lust. She was soon going to be working with Jayson Cooper, and indulging in anything, especially a fantasy, wasn't a great start to her career at ThomKnox.

That night became a night she never ever forgot. Not because of Tom or the party or the tepid New Year's kiss. No, the most memorable part of that night was meeting a handsome, blue-eyed stranger that, little did she know at the time, would soon become her husband…and soon after that, become her *ex*-husband.

One

The technology department was a big, open bullpen-style seating area with Jayson Cooper in the mix with his brethren. Gia, who'd worked in tech for years, had recently had a title update. She'd taken over as chief marketing officer after she and Jayson divorced. Her office was still on this floor, off to the side, with windows so she could look out on all of them.

Jayson didn't used to mind her being nearby.

Now, though, he *minded*.

It was closing in on a year and a half since their divorce. Moving on was difficult when the woman you were to move on *from* was directly in your line of vision day after day.

He was being looked after by a woman who'd refused to let him look after her during their entire marriage. What good was a husband whose wife refused to let him care for her?

No good, that's what.

He and Gia worked well together for their sakes as much as the sakes of their coworkers. They gave each other crap—the good-natured kind—at work and made sure to always end the day on a positive note. It'd been working… for a while.

He thought he knew how to protect and love a woman, but when it came to Gia Knox-Cooper, he'd been at sea. She was independent and headstrong and rarely if ever met him halfway. He'd known that about her going into their marriage but had expected things to change after the "I dos." Each of them had only grown further apart. Which was why their divorce had been a blessing. He understood now that were better separate.

Taylor Thompson, soon to be Taylor Knox as she was the fiancée of Royce Knox, swept into the department and past Jayson's desk.

"Coop, can you pop into Gia's office with me for a second?"

"Sure thing." He rose and followed Taylor, who was dressed smartly in a no-nonsense black dress, her dark blond hair pinned at the back of her head. She was second in charge as COO of the company, professional and spunky and exactly what Gia's oldest, most rigid brother had needed in his life. She'd sprung a pregnancy announcement on Royce last year, and now those two were to be wed. With better results, Jayson hoped, than his marriage to Gia.

Anyway, their wedding ceremony would likely include their daughter, born right after Addison and

Brannon Knox's wedding six months ago. Or, as Jayson liked to think of it, the night when he *nearly* lost his damn mind and slept with his ex-wife.

In her office, Gia was leaning back in her leather executive chair, her long dark hair spilling over her petite shoulders. Her red dress one that would make Jessica Rabbit weep with envy.

Gia was petite, curvy and hiding a beautiful body beneath that frock. It was a body he'd brought to the pinnacle of euphoria time and time again. If physical compatibility equaled a successful marriage, they'd still be together.

Taylor slapped two cream-colored notecards onto the desk and two pens on top of them. "Fill these out. Each of you."

Gia and Jayson exchanged glances before Gia picked up one of the cards to examine it more closely. "It's filled out, Tay."

"So's mine," Jayson said, picking up the other card. His name was right there. *Jayson Cooper* and beneath it, the box "attending" was marked with an X.

Taylor snatched the card from him and pointed at the blank area beneath it. "This reads 'Plus-one, yes or no' and there is a line there for a name for the seating chart."

Taylor handed the card back to him. "Yes," she said and then snapped her gaze to Gia. "Or no. This isn't twenty questions. It's *one*. I don't care what the answer is, but I need a final headcount for the caterer."

He narrowed his eyes at Gia and she mimicked his reaction.

"I'm a yes," she answered cheerily, marking the box

with a flourish. "But as my date's a celebrity, he'd rather not have the catering staff know his name." She handed over the card, her smile forced, Jayson guessed, for his benefit.

"Really?" Taylor asked, proving this was news to her. "We'll talk later. What about you, Coop?"

"Same situation," he answered, marking the yes box. "Ironically."

Gia crinkled her nose, but he kept his gaze trained on Taylor.

"There. Now was that so hard?" Taylor offered a saccharine-sweet smile and then spun on one heel and left the office.

"Holy Bridezilla," Gia said once she was gone. "She's my best friend and I love her, but *yikes*." Then she looked at him. "I didn't know you had a date."

"I didn't know you had a date, either." Going for casual, he tucked his hands in his pockets and waited.

Silence invaded for a few uncomfortable seconds while she examined her fingernails.

"Well, I didn't want to attend my other brother's wedding and have a repeat of what happened at Bran's." She then fidgeted with a pen. "That was a mistake."

Her pulling him into a spare bedroom at the mansion and kissing him so hard he saw stars was a *big* mistake and she wasn't the only one who thought so. Since then he'd had trouble keeping his mind on work and keeping their aboveboard banter from crossing into sexual territory.

His mind returned again and again to the way she'd tasted that night—like champagne, and a woman he hadn't had a sampling of for too long. If there was one essence he was powerless against it was the rare and intoxicating flavor of his ex-wife.

They'd made out hot and heavy, hiding in the spare guest bedroom after the wedding. Her dress was rucked up to her waist while she plunged her hand down his pants. The memory of the heat, the *want* and the sheer high of being able to take her where she needed to go was a memory that hadn't faded for him in the least.

He clasped his hands in front of his crotch to hide his reaction, and forced his thoughts on what had interrupted them that night.

Taylor's going-into-labor screech.

There. Thinking of that helped quell the lust.

"I didn't realize you were seeing anyone," Gia said, obviously fishing for details. Details she wouldn't get since Jayson didn't actually have a date. He guessed now he'd have to find someone. A celebrity apparently, since he'd coat-tailed Gia's story with a story of his own. He sure as shit wasn't admitting he lied to save face.

"It's new," he answered. "I didn't realize you were seeing anyone either." He'd stayed similarly single. Work kept him busy, but even if it hadn't he had no interest in a relationship. Once bitten…

Last fall he'd attended Bran's wedding alone, not thinking a thing of it. Jayson was still considered family outside of the office. Bran and Royce were like brothers. That said, even if he'd had one, bringing a date to a Knox family gathering would have been strange for him and stranger for his date.

It hadn't occurred to him until now that Gia might have a date for *this* wedding. He'd assumed she was following the same unwritten rule: no bringing dates around the ex.

Guess not.

"The tablet update is nearing release," he said, guiding the conversation back to the safe, neutral ground of ThomKnox. Where he and Gia were concerned, work might well be the last frontier of neutral territory. They'd had their differences in the past—namely him working hard to make her happy and her resisting his every effort—but here they had the same goal.

ThomKnox was the number one priority in their lives. They'd always do what was best for the company.

And, in this case, he thought as he took a seat to tell her about the latest software update in detail, the best thing for the company was Gia and him getting along.

Together or not.

Two

This is crazy.

You're crazy.

We're both crazy!

But oh, did Jay taste good. Really damn good. After being without sex for so long, Gia was beginning to worry about ill effects. She'd gone on a few random dates over the summer, since not dating would be admitting she wasn't over her ex, but each of those dates had ended with a good-night kiss that had only made her think of Jayson Cooper. So while he was totally over her, evidently she was still affected by him.

Case in point.

His tongue, though. Who could deny how good he

was with it? Either tangling with hers or gliding down her neck. He suckled on her pulse point while his fingers lifted her dress to do what he was best at: pleasure her.

Fingers in her panties, he slipped along her folds, driving her wild. She moaned into his mouth. He kissed her harder, trying to quiet her. Possibly the only part crazier than carrying on with him was doing it in her parents' vineyard mansion after her brother's wedding. When she saw the guests filtering outside, either to leave or enjoy cocktails around the fire, she'd rushed him into the nearest spare room.

No one had noticed them missing. Nor would they if she could keep her *moaning* to a minimum. A challenge, given his touch was sending her into an orgasmic stupor.

It didn't take long.

She gripped his shoulders hard, pulled her mouth from his and came. She allowed herself a breath or two before her hand was shakily finding its way to his pants. She had his belt undone, zipper down, and was cradling several inches of his budding erection when it happened.

A scream of pain shattered the air—coming from the back patio and from, she guessed, a very pregnant Taylor.

Jayson snapped his mouth from Gia's, blinking hard as if trying to focus. She held her breath and listened. A going-into-labor Taylor shouted again.

Talk about a buzzkill.

"Damn," he said, which is probably what Gia would

have said had she been able to speak after her powerful release.

And, oh, was her orgasm a good one. She'd been in
charge of her own pleasure since she and her ex went
kaput. It was irksome to be reminded of what she'd
been missing.

"Get dressed, G," he said, his raspy voice dancing
along her nerve endings. He moved her hand out of his
pants, flashed her a smile that made her knees weaker,
and then kissed her palm.

"What did we do?" she muttered. There was no good
end to this night if they slept together, intellectually
she'd known that. Yet look how close they'd come to
actually sealing the deal!

What was she thinking?

She *wasn't* thinking. Plain and simple...

Gia, chin in her palm, eyes unfocused and gazing
into the distance, blinked back to reality.

Her blue cheese–stuffed-olive dirty martini was
half gone, but then she'd arrived at the bar early on
purpose. She hadn't intended on daydreaming about
her ex-husband, or reminding herself that she'd been
without an orgasm of that caliber in over six months.
She'd arrived early and drunk down half a martini for
one reason: she needed to bolster her confidence before meeting her celebrity date.

Blinking the bar into focus, she sucked in a breath
and blew it out. Other couples dotted the room, drinks
in front of them, the low candles on the table setting
the tone: romantic. Why did she choose someplace this
romantic? She should have invited him to coffee...

Denver "Pip" Pippen, skateboarding superstar and hot cult god, was about to be interviewed for the role of a lifetime: to be her date to Royce's and Taylor's wedding.

Not that he knew that.

No, she hadn't had a date when she'd marked the RSVP card. But, with Jayson standing there looking as gorgeous and distracting as ever, she realized that attending another wedding without a date could land her in the guest bedroom with him again.

That.

Could not.

Happen.

She'd found Pip's profile on Divinely Yours, a dating app for the wealthy and elite. Not quite A-listers, but not D either. The app was recommended to her about a year ago by a well-meaning friend. At the time she'd shrugged it off, too focused on the ThomKnox tablet launch to dream of throwing herself to the wolves on a dating app. But after filling out Taylor's RSVP card under duress, Gia decided that the dating app might not be the worst idea ever.

Tonight, she'd find out.

She spotted Denver the moment he breezed through the entrance. He carried with him a certain amount of charisma that turned more than her head. As the hostess walked him over, Gia tested her own reaction. She'd seen photos, and videos, online, but this was Denver Pippen in the flesh. That was always a different experience.

His longish dark blond hair was messy and wavy. He wore a baggy T-shirt and jeans—casual but designer, and Converse sneakers. He shot her a smile that took up most of his face in the most charming way imaginable.

Yes. He'd do nicely.

"You must be Pip," she said, offering her hand.

She hadn't expected a demure kiss to the hand and wasn't disappointed. Instead he said her first name, dragging it into a prolonged "Jee-ahh" and kissed her on the cheek.

When he backed away she noticed the silver scar on his eyebrow, and another on his upper lip. She knew from videos of his skateboarding stunts that Denver also had plenty of scars on his upper arms and calves. Somehow, on him, the messy hair and scar combo worked.

"Fancy place." His lazy speech was half surfer dude and half stoner.

"I ordered already. I'm terribly impatient." She fingered the stem of her martini.

"Rad." He flagged down a waitress and ordered a beer. He was polite and brought forth a genuine smile from the waitress. *Nice.* Had he been rude, Gia would have had to leave and gone back to square one. He was doing well so far.

"So, ThomKnox. Computers. Cell phones. All that techy stuff." He wiggled his fingers as if he were talking about sorcery instead.

"That's the gist of it."

"What's your jam over there?"

"I run the marketing department."

"Rad."

She sipped her martini, hiding a smile. *Rad*, indeed.

She'd always thought that with her MIT degree she'd be *running* the tech team, but that position had gone to Jay.

Her father had assured her that Jayson was the right fit, and that he'd preferred Gia to be in a higher position, one of more prestige at ThomKnox. But when Jack's own CEO position had come up for grabs, Gia was content to let her brothers duke it out. Literally, as it were.

Newly divorced, she'd cashed in on another interest and opted to run Marketing instead. On good days she stood behind her decision to nurture her need to lie low. On bad days, she wished she'd insisted on taking over the department she loved.

Pip rapped his knuckles on their table to the beat of the music and drew her from her musings. With her eyes, she traced the scars on his hands.

"How did skateboarding become a passion?" she asked.

"My dad bought me a board when I was twelve. He used to do it. He was killer. Once I landed my first big jump, I was hooked." He held up one injured hand, where his middle finger bent at an unnatural angle. "Never deterred by danger."

"I guess not." From what she'd read on his Wikipedia page, Denver Pippen had broken bones. A lot of them. "Once I crashed, I'd be done. I'm not much of a risk taker."

She winced at the truth behind that admission, recalling the way she'd ducked out of the tech department after the divorce. She'd loved her job, but after she and Jayson split she couldn't bear to be "under" his authority another second. She needed space, and while she didn't have it in physical form, since her office was still on the tech floor, at least they weren't quibbling over who ran the weekly meetings.

"Why would you risk ruining those beautiful brains?" Denver flipped his palm over and motioned for her hand. Intrigued, she slipped her hand into his. Rough. Calloused. "I looked you up. MIT, smarty-pants. You're the prize Knox. So why'd you swipe on my mug on Divinely Yours?"

Good question. She'd waded through a sea of billionaires, millionaires, actors and video game creators. Pip was wildly different from someone she would normally choose—different from who anyone would choose for her. Pip was a guy who would be a good short-term solution to a problem. Since she wasn't ready to submerge herself entirely into the dating pool, she figured he'd be a perfectly good date to the wedding. He wouldn't have the wrong impression about how serious they were, and he'd likely walk away without looking back.

Instead of telling him he was a convenient solution, she went with a more palatable answer. "I liked your face."

He grinned. It was a handsome face.

"I like your face, too, *Jee-ahh.* So what's up? Drinks on a Monday at six o'clock? This screams trial." He drank from his beer glass. "What's the real gig?"

He was sharper than he wanted others to believe. And direct.

She lifted an eyebrow. "Now who's the smarty-pants?"

His laugh was a low, rolling chuckle.

She held on to the stem of her martini glass and told him the truth. "I need a date for my brother's wedding. It's next Saturday."

"And you thought of me?" Humor radiated off him. "You want to piss off your parents or make someone jealous?"

She wasn't trying to make Jayson jealous. Nor did she care if her parents were upset by her attending solo or with a date. What she did care about was the seemingly undeniable lure of her ex-husband.

The way Jay could look at her from across a room and make her heart skip a beat and her brain forget their checkered past. An innocent, polite dance at the last wedding reception had turned into more when his hand moved to her lower back and he'd laid his lips against her ear.

She couldn't let that happen again.

"A bit of both," she lied to her date.

"I'm your guy." Pip held up his beer glass in a toast.

He wasn't, not permanently, but he'd fill a much-needed void. Smiling, Gia tapped her glass with his.

Three

The woman lying in the sand was tall, given the way her limbs splayed attractively into a pose as she leered at the camera lens.

Gia's claim she was dating a celebrity had given Jayson an idea. He'd called his stepbrother, Mason, later that day and, as luck had it, learned that Mas had a photoshoot scheduled with a supermodel.

Cha-ching.

Mason squatted in the sand in front of the woman and gave her commands like "sultry, now sweet, give me a smile" while the shutter clicks from his camera fired.

Jayson had heard enough teasing over the years to last a lifetime. *Mason and Jayson, are you two twins or something?* The answer was obvious just by looking. Jayson had a wider, thicker build than his brother. Mason was tall and slim, with an added four inches of height. They'd both had goatees years ago, but Jayson had abandoned his. Now he either shaved or didn't and those were the only two options.

"Beautiful, Natasha," Mason praised the model as he lowered his camera. *Beautiful Natasha* was an apt nickname. The bikini-clad goddess with sand stuck to her boobs had graced many a magazine. She was on the cover of last year's *Sports Illustrated* swimsuit edition. This year she'd been replaced on the cover, but was still featured inside, and today she was shooting her own calendar.

Landing *the* Natasha Tovar was a big win for Mas. He'd started his career taking family portraits, made a brief foray as a wedding photographer—Jayson and Gia's wedding, actually—and then Mason had stumbled into shooting models, which was harder than one might imagine in California.

"We have it?" Natasha brushed sand from her supple body before slipping on a white "robe," for lack of a better term.

Jayson could see right through it and when the cups of her bikini top wet the robe, they were a pair of fluorescent orange globes he had trouble looking away from.

"Who's this?" She toweled her hair and walked every inch of her mostly legs body toward Jayson.

"This is my brother, Jayson Cooper. Goes by Cooper." Mason slanted a glance from Natasha to Jayson, his eyebrows winging upward as if to say *I told you she was perfect.*

"Nice to meet you, Cooper." She extended a hand, which he accepted. She left sand in his palm. She didn't introduce herself and Jayson figured it was because she didn't have to. He possessed a penis therefore he should know who she was. She excused herself and walked up the beach toward a trailer.

"She's putting that wiggle into her walk for you," Mason said. He thumbed through some of the shots on his Canon while the lighting guy left behind his umbrellas and reflector panels to seek out the food truck parked in front of the more populated part of the beach. "You hungry?"

"Always," Jayson said.

"That food truck sucks—" Mason tipped his head to indicate the direction his lighting guy went "—but I brought Chester's homemade tamales."

Jayson's stomach roared. Mason's husband made the best tamales on the planet. "I am not above eating half your lunch. Especially if Ches made it."

"He's a keeper." Mason smiled.

At eighteen years old, after he graduated high school, Mason had come out officially. Jayson's response? A nonchalant shrug. He couldn't have been less surprised.

Mason's father, Albert, was alarmed, which helped Jayson realize that his stepfather rarely paid attention to life outside of work. But, Albert was also a good man and, while it took him longer, he accepted that his son was gay. Jayson's mom, Julia, was as unsurprised as Jayson. She'd helped Albert realize the truth: Mason was still Mason, no matter who he loved.

Anyway, that was ancient history. Mason and Chester had wed two years ago and were now like any boring married couple. Or, what Jayson thought a boring married couple should be like. He and Gia hadn't made it to "boring."

The brothers split a pan of tamales—thankfully, Mason had two forks—while sitting on a piece of driftwood watching the waves crash on the shore. Not a bad way to spend an afternoon.

"Can't believe you drove all this way to meet her. You must be desperate," Mason said around a final bite.

Jayson tossed his fork on the empty pan and swiped his teeth with his tongue. How to respond to that? Mason knew Jay needed a wedding date—an impressive one—but Jay hadn't told him why.

He hadn't shared with his brother that he'd brought Gia to orgasm six months ago and since then she'd shut him out like it'd never happened. It wasn't unlike right before their divorce hearing, when they'd had car sex. Unplanned, mind-blowing car sex. Then, five days later, Gia showed up at court with ice in her veins like she hadn't felt the earth move.

But mind-blowing car sex could not a marriage save. Whenever they were arguing, and that became more and more often near the end, she claimed she couldn't be with someone who "controlled" her. Jayson, whose real father had controlled their household with fists and fear, never reacted well to that accusation.

"Want to tell me why you need a supermodel as your wedding date?" Mason asked.

Well. What the hell.

"Gia is bringing a date to her brother Royce's wedding. I'm not showing up alone."

"How mature."

"Gia and I almost had sex not that long ago, Mas." Jayson shook his head. "Could have set us back years. Plus, the guy's famous. I had to step up."

"Famous?"

"Denver Pippen," Jayson said through his teeth. Apparently, Gia had met him for cocktails and things went well. Not that Jayson had been lurking around the office, but okay, he'd been *sort of* lurking. And he'd heard Gia excitedly telling Taylor that her date was going to be none other than skateboarding legend, Denver "Pip" Pippen.

"He's hot," Mason said. "That sports drink commercial where he leaps those cars…"

"Not helping." Jayson stood, frustrated. "What could Gia possibly have in common with a guy who's broken nearly every bone in his body? She's all brains and he pounds his into the pavement."

"And you thought Natasha would make her as jealous as you are." Mason smirked.

"I'm not jealous of that joker-smile idiot." He frowned, considering. "But if I see him kiss Gia, I'm going to give him a new scar."

Mason laughed. "It's past time you *both* got out there, Coop. You've been out of the game for a while."

"Thanks for the reminder." He pushed a hand through his hair. "It's not easy to date when your ex-wife is in your social circles."

Mason gave his brother the side-eye. "You two *stay* in each other's circles. You still act married. Divorced people move on. You two moved sideways."

Jayson shook his head, but he wasn't committed to

it. Mason had a point. It wasn't easy to move on when the wound was fresh.

"I'm moving on now," Jay said, simply because he needed to say it out loud.

"Good. I've been priming Natasha today about your arrival. Told her you were hot and single. Then I mentioned that you were going to the Knox family vineyard over the weekend and you should have seen her face." Mason reached for his camera. "Actually you *can* see her face. I snapped a few shots of her reaction."

"You did tell her I needed her to be a plus-one to a wedding, didn't you?"

"And do all the legwork for you? Absolutely not. Natasha!" Mason called over his shoulder.

Her trailer door opened a crack. "More photos?"

"No photos. Cooper has something to ask you." Mas slapped Jay's shoulder as Natasha came out of the trailer and wiggled her way across the sand. "No time like the present."

Mason vanished inside and shut the door behind him.

Natasha, still in her see-through robe, peered up at Jayson expectantly. "What's up, Coop?"

Palming the back of his neck, Jayson smiled down at the supermodel. Here went nothing. "Are you busy on Saturday?"

Four

Denver drove separately to the wedding, which left Gia wringing her hands. She assumed he knew better than to wear a baggy T-shirt, jeans and Converse to a formal Knox event but...*did he?*

Her own attire was a blush pink bridesmaid's dress, short but flowy. The dress was higher in the front than the back, the spaghetti straps showing off her shoulders. The narrow bodice gave her a bit too much cleavage, but it wasn't as if she could help it.

Turned out there was no need to worry. Denver showed up for the wedding in head-to-toe Armani so it wasn't hard to forgive his windblown hair with sunglasses perched in it. He turned plenty of heads upon his arrival, mostly other men at the party who knew sports.

She hadn't spotted Jayson yet, but no matter. She'd achieved her goal. She was at Royce and Taylor's wedding with a date, which meant she wasn't going to trip over Jayson after she drank too much champagne and then try to take his pants off.

Denver made his way to the white folding chairs set up on the hill overlooking a stunning vineyard and Gia readied herself with the other bridesmaid, her very pregnant sister-in-law Addison.

Addi blew out a breath and gave Gia a steady smile. "I'm fine."

"It'd serve Taylor right if you went into labor right here, right now," Gia joked. After all it was Taylor who'd gone into labor after Addison's wedding.

"I'll see what I can do," Addi said with a laugh.

The violinist started playing. As maid of honor Gia began the procession of two. She stepped onto the white runner, smiling for the photographer. She winked at her brother Royce who looked uncharacteristically nervous, before her eyes tracked to Brannon who gave her a nod.

When her gaze naturally reached the final groomsman, her heart thundered. Of course she knew that Jayson was a groomsman and would be standing with her brothers, but she wasn't ready for the gut-punch vision of him at the end of an aisle she was walking. They'd been married outside as well, though their wedding was beachfront instead of among a backdrop of grapevines.

Her smile tightened along with her grip on the bouquet of lilacs. She could do this. She would. For her brother.

Positioned up front, she scanned the crowd for her

date, finding Denver sitting in full man-spread in the second row. Before she could decide how she felt about that, Addison took her place next to Gia and Taylor began her descent.

Taylor made an ethereal bride in white, the short beaded train of her dress shimmering in the midday sunshine. Tears pricked Gia's eyes as she watched her best friend take Royce's hand, and they rolled down her cheeks as she considered that her best friend was about to become her *sister.*

Once Royce had kissed his bride, and Addison and Gia had gone through several tissues, the crowd cheered for the latest Mr. and Mrs. Knox. The exit music began, which meant Gia was officially off the hook.

Or so she thought.

Brannon bypassed her to take Addi's arm. "Sorry for the bait and switch, sis, but my wife needs me."

"You wish," Gia teased. Addison chuckled.

Addison, her hand bracing her very pregnant belly, beamed up at her husband before looping her arm in his. Bran mumbled something to her and she nodded, assuring him she was "still fine."

"Stuck with me, then," Jay commented as he offered Gia his arm.

"The sacrifices we make for those we love," she mumbled before pausing to smile for the photographer. "I didn't see your date."

"She's seated behind your date."

Gia turned her head to find her date leaning over a chair and chatting up a gorgeous brunette. She had to blink twice to be sure she was seeing correctly. "Is that—"

"Natasha Tovar. Supermodel."

Yes, that's what Gia thought. She let out a noncommittal hum. "Did Mason hook you up with Miss *Sports Illustrated*?"

"He introduced us. She likes my accent." He leaned down when he spoke. Whenever he was close, she had trouble thinking clearly.

"You don't have an accent."

"To Natasha I do. She's Russian."

"Good for her," Gia grumbled.

The guests meandered to the tent next and Gia and Jayson waited for their dates. As the supermodel approached, Gia felt her lip curl.

It'd have made her day if Natasha Tovar had been airbrushed within an inch of her life in her photos, but the gorgeous brunette was every bit as tantalizing in person as on a glossy magazine page. She was tall and leggy with high cheekbones and big eyes. Every other step she took revealed one supple thigh through the slit in her short black dress.

"What about your guy?" Jay rumbled, his voice low. "Does he own a hairbrush or is that how the kids are wearing it these days?"

Jerking her attention to Denver, who she honestly hadn't been watching, Gia retorted, "I admit, it's nice to date someone younger after having been with an older man for so long."

Jay smirked, his confidence unwavering. "Aged to perfection, sweetheart."

Goose bumps cropped up on her forearms the way

they did whenever her ex-husband was accidentally sexy. Which happened more than she'd dare admit. Thankfully their dates reached them before he noticed her reaction.

"Dude, do you know who this is?" Denver asked Gia, his thumb pointing at Natasha.

"Ms. Tovar, is it?" Gia extended a hand. "It's lovely to meet you. I didn't know you were dating our Jayson."

"Coop and I met a few days ago and we hit it off. He's not gay like his brother so it worked out."

Gia pressed her lips together to smother a laugh and turned to Jayson. "Such high praise."

"Looks like Denver has all of his teeth," Jayson said under his breath. "Good for you."

Gia leered at him but he still wore that infuriatingly handsome smirk. He swept Natasha away and Gia groused in their wake, wishing they didn't look good together. They did. Dammit.

"She's hot," Denver put in as he placed his hand on her lower back.

"Not all of us are built like giraffes," she said, noting that she was being catty but not really caring.

"No, baby, not you." Denver bent his knees to come eye to eye with her, his hands gripping her biceps while he looked straight into her eyes. "You are gorgeous in another way. A different league. Beneath this package of curvaceous goodness, you deliver a totally gnarly experience."

Judging by his smile that was a compliment. "Um. Thanks?"

"You're welcome. Let's find some grub." She and Denver walked to the reception tent overlooking the vineyard. Where Addi and Bran's wedding had been contained to the immediate backyard, Taylor and Royce's was more sprawling. There were easily three times the number of guests here than at Bran and Addi's. Maybe Gia would be lucky and she wouldn't run into Jayson and Natasha again tonight.

Alas, when Denver and Gia approached the bar, Jayson was there, handing off a slim glass of clear bubbly liquid with a lime wedge in it to Natasha.

"What do you think, baby? Shots?" Denver asked Gia. Jayson turned and frowned. No, not a frown. There was an entire lightning storm forming behind his eyes.

Ignoring them both, she ordered for herself. "Dirty martini, up with three olives. Blue cheese stuffed if you have them."

"Shot of rum and a bitter IPA. Something local if ya got it." Denver seemed none the wiser to Jayson's disapproving presence.

Well, her ex could just deal with it. She didn't like his date any more than he liked hers.

The bartender made their drinks and Jayson, one hand wrapped around a glass of red wine, the other around Natasha's waist, gestured to a table.

"Dirty martini," Natasha laughed before she walked off with Jayson.

"What the hell was that supposed to mean?" Gia whispered to herself.

"It means she knows you got it going on, baby," her date answered.

"Gia," she snapped, shooting lasers from her eyes at Denver. "My name is Gia."

"Jee-ahh." His grin widened.

She sighed. She guessed that was better than "baby."

Five

"The guest rooms are on the second floor," Gia was saying to Denver as they crested the stairs. It was getting late, most of the guests filtering off. As part of the bridal party, it was her duty to oversee that the guests who were staying the night had everything they needed.

"Cool. I'll grab my stuff." He dropped a kiss on her mouth—one that startled her since they hadn't kissed yet. The night they'd enjoyed their first drink together had ended the way it'd started: with a demure brush of his lips on her cheek. "Yo, Natasha," Denver called before jogging up the stairs.

Gia's eyes sank closed. *Of course* the Russian goddess had witnessed that kiss. She turned, unsurprised to find Jayson there as well.

"We are staying, too," Natasha informed Gia.

"Yippee."

"Yes, it's very exciting," Natasha said, missing Gia's sarcasm. "I'll freshen up, but not done yet. More dancing." She gave Jayson a limp shove on the chest and then glided up the stairs.

"Enjoying yourselves?" Gia asked him, her tone flat.

"I love a good wedding." He pushed his hands into his pants pockets. He'd lost the jacket and bowtie from earlier, which left him in a white button-down shirt with the sleeves pushed to his elbows.

He looked good.

He rarely didn't.

He cleared his throat. "Where's your room?"

"Far end of the hallway." Denver's room was catty-corner to hers, not that she volunteered that information. "What about yours?"

"We're in the middle." He shot her a heated look and she could've sworn it was because he was thinking of the room they'd stayed in when they'd last visited her parents' mansion. The master guest suite. At least neither of them had been stationed there tonight.

Still, the "we" niggled at her. "We" meant that he'd be crawling into bed with *Miss Russia* tonight.

"She's not your type." Gia worked to sound curious. To be fair, she *was* curious. She hadn't seen him with anyone since they divorced and then he came out of the gate with a thoroughbred.

His shrug was infuriatingly blasé. "I don't have a type."

Her type used to be broad, dark and handsome with a protective streak a mile and a half wide. Five o'clock shadow and short-cropped dark hair. Eyes so blue she'd felt as if her soul was being inspected by a fallen angel…

But that was when she was in love with Jayson. She wasn't in love with him anymore.

When she'd married him she thought he understood her; that he'd allow her to be herself and forge her own way. Instead he'd attempted to corral and protect her, a lot like her father and brothers had done.

She twisted her lips in thought. "I don't have a type either."

"Coop! I found these in our room!" Natasha jogged down the stairs waving a pair of maracas from a Knox family trip to Puerto Rico. A keepsake. Gia felt the slow burn of anger broil her hairline. This woman needed to learn keep her hands off what didn't belong to her.

"Hey!" Gia lifted her voice, "Those are—"

"Going right back to where they came from." Jayson removed the maracas from Natasha's hands and gave them to Gia. As he walked off with his date, Gia heard him assure Natasha that they'd find some other way to entertain themselves on the dance floor.

And probably, Gia thought as she stomped upstairs, they'd find a way to entertain themselves in their shared bed, too.

Ugh.

"Cool digs." Denver shut his bedroom door and met her in the hallway Then he rubbed his hands together. "What are those for?"

"Nothing." Gia shoved the maracas into his chest

and bypassed him to walk into his room. "Change of plans. We're staying in my room."

She exited carrying his duffel bag and opened the door to her room next. He followed behind her, a confused expression on his face.

"Together?" he asked.

"Yeah." She dropped his bag onto the down comforter. "Together."

Denver gave her one of his wide, carefree grins. "Sweet."

"But dancing is my *favorite*."

It wasn't Natasha's enunciation of favorite (fave-oh-right) that annoyed Jayson so much as the whine that accompanied it.

She was a beautiful woman with scads of confidence. She was educated and outgoing. She didn't drink alcohol. She was polite to everyone she met.

But.

She was needy and clingy and driving him up the wall. He'd danced with her. And danced. *And danced.*

He unwound his date's fingers from his forearm. "Natasha. No means no."

She thrust out her bottom lip. It didn't make her any less attractive.

He offered a tolerant smile and gentled his voice. "If I don't have a cigar with Brannon, he's going to kick my ass."

She let out a sharp gasp. "Cigars cannot touch this mouth."

"It's just one," he said, instead of *so, what?* There wasn't a single spark of attraction between them, though sleeping with her had crossed his mind. If for no other reason than to take his mind off his ex-wife, who was swishing around here in a short dress with enough cleavage to fall into.

He'd bet Denver noticed. Jayson sawed his teeth together.

"No kissing," Natasha hissed before she scampered off. The band played a fast song and she grabbed hold of a geriatric gentleman and started dancing with him. Jayson seemed to remember that guy from a board meeting. Anyway, the old guy looked happier than Jay was about the dancing, so they could have at it.

Outside, he found Bran standing in a half circle with a few other guys from work.

"There he is." Bran handed over a cigar and cutter. "Where's your supermodel date? Did she finally realize what a loser you were and ditch you?"

"She's dancing." *Some more.*

"Gia and Denver Pippen?" Bran asked around the cigar between his teeth. "What's that about?"

Jayson cut and lit his own cigar. He took a long puff and blew out his answer. "Wish I knew."

"Haven't seen them in a while. Did they leave?"

Jayson welded his back teeth together. "I think they're staying."

More like he *knew* they were staying. At the end of the hall. He saw her go upstairs earlier. If she'd met Denver in that room, Jayson had a good idea what they were doing right now.

He shouldn't care, but when it came to Gia, married or not, he'd always had the fierce desire to protect her. Denver seemed harmless—the sports star probably did more damage to himself than he'd ever do to another person—but she might need a reminder that she didn't have to wander that far down the evolutionary scale to rummage up a date.

"Huh." Bran sent a derisive look at the second floor of the house where a few bedroom lights were on. Gia's brother didn't go on a rant about her and Denver, and Jayson understood. Bran was close friends with Jay, had been for years, but if he had to choose sides, Bran would choose Gia. That was the way it should be.

"How's Addi? She holding on to that baby a while longer?" Jayson asked, segueing as seamlessly as possible.

"She's taking it easy tonight. Other than a few kicks to the beat of the music, she says the baby is content to wait." Bran's smile was contagious. "God, I can't wait to meet her. My daughter."

"Me too." Jay slapped him heartily on the shoulder. Brannon and Royce were family. Being divorced from Gia hadn't changed that. After they'd split, she'd insisted no one treat Jayson differently. The only one unable to follow that request was Gia herself. She'd been aloof and cool for the most part. Exception being at this very house about six months ago…

"Gentlemen," Royce greeted them upon his approach. He was still dressed in his tux, the formality suiting him. Taylor, in her formfitting lace wedding gown, a scooped V in the front and back, wore a tired smile.

"Cigar?" Bran offered Taylor.

"Shut up." She gave her brother-in-law a playful slap

before fussing with a drooping ring of flowers in her hair. "I'm falling apart."

"You're not," Jayson assured her.

"Thanks, Coop." She smiled genuinely before turning her attention to Bran. "Say the word and we'll delay the honeymoon. Royce and I want to be home when Addi has the baby."

Jayson was surprised to see Royce nod his agreement. "It's not a problem, Bran. Really."

"Go." Bran waved a hand. "The baby will be here when you come back."

"But I want to be there." Taylor appeared as unsatisfied by this decision as her new husband. "The *moment* it happens."

"Guys. Go to the Bahamas. Any excuse to delay and neither of you will ever go. You work too much."

Jayson regarded the ground and smiled to himself. Bran was as dedicated to their family's company as Royce and Taylor, even though he played down his commitment.

"He's right," Taylor told Royce. "Plus, if we stay here, your mom and dad will insist on keeping their granddaughter anyway. They've been looking forward to our honeymoon as much as we have."

"Not as much," Royce told his bride.

"We have things under control here," Jayson assured her. He was happy for them. Not every marriage ended in catastrophe.

Though a lot of them do, murmured the cynic inside.

"*Fine.* I'll go to the Bahamas," she said with a surly huff. "Where is Gia, anyway? I wanted to say goodbye."

This again? "I believe she went to bed."

"Oh." Taylor's brow crinkled. Jayson was an inch away from encouraging her to go upstairs and interrupt whatever might be happening, but he managed to keep that request to himself.

Progress. He was growing.

Royce shook Jayson's then Brannon's hands. "Call us the second Addi's in the hospital," he instructed his brother. "Day or night."

"Honeymoon, Royce," Bran told him. "You have to relax."

"I don't relax." Royce dipped his chin at Jayson, his tone firmer than before. "Coop. Keep an eye on our girl."

"What was that about?" Bran asked once they'd gone.

"No idea," Jayson lied, lifting his cigar to his lips.

Royce wasn't referring to his daughter, but Gia.

It wasn't so long ago that Gia's father, Jack Knox, had given Jayson a similar command. Her family had always wanted to protect her.

It'd taken Jayson a while to learn it, but he now knew what Gia wanted more than anything. And that was to take care of herself.

Six

Last January, the ThomKnox parking garage

"Thanks for the help," Gia said, chasing after Jayson. "Even though I told you I'd carry that."

"Not happening, G." Like he'd let her carry a thirty-six-inch screen from the executive floor down to the parking garage. "Why are you in the garage, anyway? You should be parked up front in the space with your name on it."

She beeped a key fob. "My interior is black leather. It'd soak up the heat from the sun and then when I climbed in I'd suffocate and die."

"Well, we can't have that." The black Mercedes Benz C-Class was a beauty. He should know. He'd picked it out. At the time he hadn't imagined he'd be leaving it with her because they were divorcing.

Five days from now they'd finalize their split on paper. Officially.

He'd already secured an apartment. Most of what he was taking there was already in storage. He'd moved out gradually, thinking it would hurt less. Turned out there was no way for divorce to hurt less. It hurt. That's all there was to it.

He slid the large screen, in its factory box, into the trunk and shut it. She went around to the driver's seat and climbed inside, turning over the engine. The sound echoed in the garage. Not a soul was parked on the third level. Other than a guard and few brown-nosers, Jay guessed the first floor was just as empty.

Gia rolled down the window. "Guess I'll see you later."

He locked onto her brown eyes, stuck on what to say about any of it. All of the arguments he wished could have been simple misunderstandings. All of the accusations said in the heat of the moment that he should have taken back.

Too late now.

"I'm sorry," he said, the words exiting his throat like broken glass. Not because he didn't mean it. He was sorry, sorry that their marriage was ending in a stalemate.

"Don't be." Her smile was forced. "We did our best."

"Did we?"

She watched him, chewing on her lip. He hadn't meant to ask, but now that he had...*did they* do their best? Or were they giving up?

She shut off the engine and stepped out, folding her arms and leaning on the door. Eyes on his, she said, "Yes. We did."

"I'm not a quitter. Neither are you," he offered. "This feels like quitting."

"We can't change the past, Jay." She shrugged. "And the future is unknown. Besides, we're not quitting. We're deciding to be apart. Our love for this company, and my family, isn't going anywhere. The only difference in our lives will be that you no longer live in the house."

He rested a hand on the car's roof and hovered over her. "I'll also no longer be in your bed."

Heat warmed her caramel-colored eyes to deep, chocolate brown. He brushed her soft cheek with the back of his fingers.

"I'll no longer kiss these lips good-night." He touched her mouth with his thumb. That would be the hardest transition—for both of them, he'd bet.

"We have a few days," she whispered, arching her back and brushing her breasts against his chest.

He didn't need more of an invitation than that. Lowering his face, he captured her lips with his. She wrapped her arms around his neck and kissed him back.

Her entire body participated, from her fingernails scratching his scalp to her leg wrapping around his hip. Hand beneath her thigh, he hiked her leg higher and deepened their kiss. His erection raged as a contradicting voice inside yelled for him to both stop and go faster.

"Point of no return," he breathed into her ear before

nipping her earlobe. If they slept together, it'd change everything. He knew it in his bones.

He wasn't sure if that was wise, or infinitely stupid.

She pulled away, her tongue swiping her bottom lip. When her teeth came down to capture it, he knew her answer.

"One more time," she answered.

He didn't think, he only acted.

Cigar enjoyed, time killed, Jayson trudged upstairs to his date.

He'd waited until the band packed up, sitting up and talking to Bran and a few of his friends to further stall the inevitable. He knew Gia was upstairs with Denver. Neither of them had reappeared. Jayson hadn't been in a big hurry to run upstairs and corroborate that suspicion.

He turned down the hallway to walk to his room when Denver clomped up the stairs behind him, a glass of brown liquid in hand. "One for the road, bro," he said, his speech wobbly.

Jayson welded his jaw together as Denver disappeared into Gia's room. Fists balled, he considered his options. Bust into the room and demand his ex-wife stay away from that harebrained, brick-headed dolt, or stand idly by.

There would be consequences if he banged on that door and checked up on her. She didn't like him undermining her. That was the word she'd often used. *Undermining.* As if protecting someone he loved was an insult.

Then again, making sure she was safe was worth

any consequence, big or small. He'd started toward the bedroom door when her laugh floated out from under it.

He froze in place, at once disgusted and resigned. She sounded fine. Happy, even.

That sucked.

On heavy legs he turned back toward his own room and walked in. Natasha was waiting for him.

"Fix it." She pointed at the dresser, where one drawer was opened at a weird slant. "I can't live like this."

"Can't have you roughing it," he said, sarcasm thick, as he fixed the drawer with a quick wiggle. Forget that she was in a Knox mansion overlooking a vineyard, majestic mountains as a backdrop.

All he wanted to do was close his eyes and wake up in the morning.

"You are not nice," she said. Arguably she was right. He hadn't been very nice. "I am showering. Don't join me." She closed herself into the bathroom. And locked the door.

"No problem, lady." He sat on the edge of the bed and scrubbed his face with both hands.

He was beat, but he couldn't sleep knowing what was going on at the end of the hallway. He decided to head downstairs. The bar was closed, but he knew where Jack kept the good scotch. Jayson needed a nip after the day he'd had. Hell, he needed a *bottle*.

When he exited his room, Gia was tiptoeing out of hers. They shut the doors to their rooms simultaneously. He smiled and she smiled back at him, each amused by the unintentional choreography.

She'd changed from her bridesmaid's dress into a short pair of cutoff shorts and an oversize pink T-shirt. She looked cute. Relaxed. Warm and sleepy.

The thought of Denver touching her made Jayson want to howl.

She shoved her hands into her back pockets. "Hey."

"Hi." Still in his trousers and white shirt from the wedding, he was overdressed for this chance meeting. "Couldn't sleep."

"Yeah. My roommate is, ah, he finally fell asleep."

After what?

He didn't dare ask.

"Is the party winding down?" She folded her arms over her stomach and shifted on her feet. Fidgeting, the way she did when she was nervous.

"Royce and Taylor took off for the honeymoon. Addi and Bran are in their room. Your mom and dad left a little while ago with the baby. Just catering staff and house staff tidying up downstairs."

She nodded, glancing away before looking back at him. "I was going to grab a snack. Want to join me?"

"I was heading for the bar, but I never turn down a meal."

She joined him at the top of the stairs and they walked down side by side. "I didn't mean to take you from your *date*."

If it wasn't for the way she pronounced that hard *T*, he wouldn't have had any idea his ex-wife was jealous. He wasn't proud of it, but he liked knowing he wasn't the only one entertaining the green-eyed monster tonight.

Downstairs in the kitchen, she weaved between the

house staff, greeting them by name while pulling out containers of leftovers from the fridge.

She handed him a large plate and filled it with a variety of salads and pasta, meats and cheeses, and on another plate served up a large slice of cake. When she started to put the containers back into the fridge, one of the house staff shooed her away.

She walked outside and on the way Jayson grabbed a pair of sparkling-water bottles. They stopped at a picnic table beneath a broad tree overlooking the vineyards. The house glowed warmly in the background, looking as homey as a thirty-something-room mansion could.

They dug into their shared snack in silence.

"Mmm. God. This is better than…" She trailed off before rephrasing her statement. "This is better than it was the first time."

"Did you do something to work up an appetite?" He narrowed his eyes.

She popped a square of cheese into her mouth and raised an eyebrow. "Did *you*?"

He reached for his water bottle and unscrewed the cap before taking a long guzzle. Not as good as scotch, but it would do. Patience shot, he said what was on his mind. "What the hell are you doing with that clown?"

"Excuse me?"

"Denver Pippen. *That's* who you're choosing to be seen with?"

"How is that any of your business?" She let out an incredulous laugh.

"I refuse to stand by while you waste your time with an idiot like Denver Pippen."

"Oh, you're one to talk! You brought a runway model to my brother's wedding."

"She's a *swimsuit* model."

Even in the dim light he could make out the redness of his ex-wife's cheeks. "You're a hypocrite. You're allowed to sleep with whoever you want, but I can't? Who the hell do you think you are?"

"I didn't sleep with Natasha," he blurted out before he thought better of it.

"Not yet," Gia said, but her voice was small. She hadn't expected him to say that.

"Not ever," he answered with finality.

Seven

Jayson took a bite of the cake and licked his fork. Gia crossed her legs beneath the table, memories of his mouth—and how good he was with it—assaulting her.

So he hadn't slept with Natasha? Gia had to chew on that for a while. She did so with a slice of brie.

He scooped up another large bite of leftover wedding cake. "Is it about sex? Is that the appeal?"

Unwilling to confess anything, she claimed her own fork and ate a bite of cake. She was still sort of in shock that Jayson hadn't slept with the beautiful woman he'd brought to the wedding.

"If it's about sex, you can do better," he pressed.

She met his eyes and in their blue depths recalled the way he used to look at her. Heated. Down to her very soul. Sex with Jayson had been exquisite. Unparalleled.

Too long ago.

"Who am I supposed to sleep with? *You*?" Her heart thundered while she held her breath. Waiting. Daring him to answer. He didn't disappoint.

"Yes. If what you're after is a physical release, I'm a sure thing. But not with some random guy who isn't worthy of you." The words were gravel dragged over concrete. Jayson was pissed. Which also made him *hot*.

If temptation was a grain of sand, she'd be standing on an island. He could deliver on a physical release— tenfold. And if any proof was needed, she had it. Her body had come alive the second he'd said the word *yes*.

But they'd learned that lesson, hadn't they?

"We tried that already," she said. "We're good in bed but not outside of it. Look at us now. We should be in our separate rooms and yet…"

"And yet." He let the words hang.

She had a heart to protect. Unraveling her marriage had been the hardest thing she'd ever done in her life. Away from him she'd finally felt like an adult who was in charge of her own life. She loved her family, but they had a way of coddling her that she didn't appreciate. She understood that she was the youngest, but her reaching the pinnacle of adulthood should have quelled everyone's urge to protect her.

The freedom of being married was eye-opening… until she'd realized Jayson trying to take care of her much like her father and brothers.

There was a certain amount of freedom that came with being single. She could eat dinner whenever she liked without having to take a vote about whether to

order out or dine in. She could stay up too late, fall
asleep on the couch, enjoy the shower all to herself…

Although that part had its downsides.

Jayson had washed her back *and* her front when
they'd lived together. In the moments she was romantic with herself, she used some of those memories as
motivation.

But.

Going backward was never the best way forward.
Wasn't that what all the memes on Pinterest said?

"It's too late." She stood from the picnic table.

He stood and blocked her path, hulking and dark,
brooding and beautiful. "Too late for what?"

She put a hand on his chest to push him away but
it settled there, content to touch him even as her brain
urged against it. "It's too late to get back together."

He leaned in, the clean scent of his aftershave mingling with the crisp air from the vineyard. Lips close
to hers, but still not touching, he muttered, "Who said
anything about getting back together?"

Time stopped.

The only sounds came from the catering staff pack-
ing up the truck and the rustling of the leaves overhead. Chaotic thoughts dipped and weaved inside her
head while she debated the very thing she shouldn't
be debating.

Was she delaying the inevitable? Or was she too
tired to think clearly?

Too *excited* to think clearly…

"You're right, G." He dragged in a sigh and blew it
out, his breath dusting her cheek as he moved his lips
to her cheek. "It's too late for this conversation."

She didn't know if he meant it was too late tonight or too late overall but either way she supposed he was right.

"Good night."

"Good night." She watched him go even though part of her wanted to chase after him. The stupid part of her that forgot what life was like when they'd been married.

He'd been opinionated and stubborn. He didn't listen when she spoke. He thought he knew best. He made decisions for her instead of with her. What made her think he'd changed?

Upstairs the light in his bedroom window turned on and then off. He was in there now, with Natasha. He hadn't slept with her. Not yet. But like with their marriage, Gia was out of time. She'd had her chance to have him for herself. And it would have been amazing.

But then what?

Inside, a staff member rushed to take the dishes from her hands. Gia headed upstairs to her date, by-passing Jayson's bedroom door and doing her best to shut out what might or might not be happening beyond it.

Denver was sprawled out and snoring, where she'd left him. She crept through the darkness and bumped into his foot hanging off the end of the bed. Grabbing her pillow, she snagged a quilt off the footboard and went to the armchair in the corner.

Looked like she'd be sleeping here tonight while Prince Charming hogged the covers.

Natasha turned pouting into an art form.

Jayson had never seen anything like it. He'd gone

back to the room last night and had tried to negotiate
for one of the pillows. She'd kept all four. He could
see the argument forming in midair between them, so
he'd smiled and assured her he was good on the floor.
Which was where he slept, his tuxedo balled up into a
makeshift pillow while he slept in his shorts.

Now morning, he was feeling every inch of that
hardwood floor on his aching lower back. He needed a
cup of coffee more than a shark needed seawater. The
outdoor patio was bustling with wedding guests who'd
stayed over. They were making their way through the
breakfast buffet and from the looks of it, the food sup-
ply was nearing depletion.

He squinted through the windows against the bright
sunshine, his eyes adjusting and catching sight of Natasha in a royal blue dress. Her plate was piled with fruit
and she was carrying a glass of green liquid.

Yeah, he'd skip socializing outside, thank you very
much.

He tipped the last of the coffee into a mug, grateful
not to have to mingle to acquire a much-needed caf-
feine fix. He couldn't talk to Natasha without at least
being mildly alert. He raised the mug to his lips, but
before the blessed moment that first hot drop hit his
tongue, Gia appeared out of the ether.

"Is that the last cup?"

She wore the same cutoff frayed shorts and pink top
from last night, only today she'd strapped on open-toed
sandals. They added to her height, which brought her
lips closer to his. At least the sandals were what he was
blaming on his inability to look away from her mouth.

"You look like you slept better than me," he told her.

She looked rested. Damned good. A little too rumpled for his pleasure, like Denver had slid his busted fingers through her hair this morning.

"There's more coffee outside." Jayson scowled and lifted the mug to his lips again. This time she wrapped her fingers around his at the handle.

"Then go outside and fetch yourself a cup. This is my house." A feral spark lit her dark eyes as she tugged on the mug.

"This is your *parents'* house. My employers. Plus, I was here first." He pulled up on the mug while she pulled down, each of them careful not to spill the precious liquid that would deliver morning pep.

"I can't go out there," she said with a frown.

"Why not?"

But then he turned his head and saw Denver lounging at the carafe, chatting to a couple Jayson didn't recognize.

"Did you two have a spat?" Jayson's smile was incurable at the idea.

"If by *spat* you mean did I sneak back into our shared room on tiptoes so I wouldn't have to wake him and have an awkward conversation this morning about how I wasn't going to sleep with him, then yes. We had a spat."

Shocked by that, he temporarily forgot to hold on to the mug. She easily removed it from his hand, doctored it with some half-and-half from the fridge and leaned on the wide, stainless steel doors. She took the first coveted sip, closed her eyes and hummed.

"You mean have an awkward conversation about how you weren't going to sleep with him *again*?"

Jayson asked, fairly sure that's not what she meant. Sounded like she hadn't slept with Pip at all. If so, *that* was good news.

"I didn't sleep with him. Do you think I'd sleep with a guy on our first date or something?"

He tilted his head and watched her with his eyebrows raised.

Cheeks blushing, she mumbled at the edge of the mug, "You don't count."

"I don't?" Hand on her waist, he leaned over her to say into her ear, "As I recall it was right in this house." Her turn to be too shocked to hold on to the coffee. He reclaimed the mug and took a heavenly drink.

"That bathroom, if memory serves." He pointed across the hall at the staircase, beyond which was a half bath where they'd sneaked off after excusing themselves from the dinner table.

"That wasn't our first date. It was a work function." Her lips lifted at the corners. Good memory for both of them, that night.

"Tomato, potato."

Smiling, she shook her head at his bad joke.

"In all seriousness—" he moved the mug when she reached for it "—I'm glad you didn't sleep with him."

"I'm glad you didn't sleep with *her*." She snatched the mug. "You didn't, right?"

He shook his head. "I didn't."

"Good. She's too beautiful. It's unfair to us mortals."

Oh, Gia. He managed a sad smile. Tipping her chin, he peered down into her coffee-colored eyes, took in the riot of deep brown waves surrounding a face he'd stared at many a night while watching her sleep. Without makeup, freckles dotted the bridge of her nose—too faint to see unless you were really looking.

He was really looking.

"She's got nothin' on you, G."

They were in a holding pattern, her hands wrapped around the mug, and one of his hands on her face, the other flattened on the refrigerator next to her shoulder. The rest of the world might as well have crumbled to dust. All his reasons for not sleeping with her were harder to grasp when he was this close to her.

If they slept together she'd throw up a wall. They'd argue. This would end as badly, if not worse, than it had when they'd divorced.

And still…

"Jay…" She was poised to say something really undesirable. Maybe a "we can't" or "we shouldn't." She would have been right.

So he did what he had to do to prevent hearing it—and kissed her before she was able to speak.

Eight

Gia wasn't sure who leaned in first and erased the gap between them, but before she knew it, the sexual tension that had been roaring inside her like a five-alarm fire in the dry season *ignited*.

Jayson's warm lips pressed against hers as her back flattened on the cool steel door of the refrigerator.

His mouth was still fused with hers when he took the coffee mug from her hands and set it on the counter. He pulled her away from the fridge and, still kissing her, walked her out of the kitchen. Had anyone seen them? Had their dates seen them? She didn't know.

She didn't *care*.

When they reached the staircase, he came up for air and craned his neck toward the voices coming from the top.

There was a moment of hesitancy that gave her enough time to reconsider, but she only laughed. He took that as a yes, when in reality it was a *hell yes*, before eagerly steering her into the bathroom on the other side of the stairs.

Having sex back where it'd all started was risky territory, but by the time he shut them into the small room, she only cared that they were finally—*blessedly*—alone. He didn't bother with the switch, so the yellow glow of a night light barely illuminated the space—if it could even be called that. His big body added to the necessary bathroom accoutrements, the only place left for her was where he put her next.

On top of the sink.

"Oh!" Hand to her mouth, she stifled her surprised reaction as the people who owned those upstairs voices passed by the bathroom door. Once they were gone, Jay moved her hand away.

Mouth ravaging hers, his hands moved to her T-shirt and stripped it over her head. He didn't hesitate, didn't ask, didn't wait. He simply read her body language and right now—with her own hands pawing at his T-shirt—it was fairly obvious what she wanted.

Him.

Her fingertips raked over his abdominal muscles, still defined the way she remembered. So much of him was the way she remembered—which was both good and bad—but at the moment she focused on the parts of him she craved.

His seeking mouth over hers.

His diving tongue, hot and insistent.

His big hands, making her delicate by comparison.

She unbuttoned his jeans and slipped her hand inside. Both of them moaned their approval when she found what she was looking for. Long and broad, he was a sight to behold. She couldn't resist sneaking a peek of her stroking hand in the meager light.

"This is a bad idea," she couldn't help pointing out. She was out of breath from excitement, no longer able to call up *why* this was a bad idea. She only knew that it was.

"The worst," he agreed. "Some things never change." A crooked, cocky smile crested his firm mouth, his eyes at half-mast while his erection was at full tilt. "That was verbatim what you said the last time we were in here about to do this for the first time."

"You remember that?" she asked as he divested her of her shorts. She had to let go of him to support herself on the edge of the sink but once her lower half was naked, she put her hands on him again.

"Are you kidding?" There was something tender in his voice, even as he wrestled with her shoes and shorts. Something about his tone reminded her of how in love they once were. Before he became the Fixer of All Things.

"I—I don't have a condom," she said since that was the first unromantic comment that popped into her head.

"I do." He frowned. "In my room."

She shook her head. "We're not risking that again."

Being busted by Addison at her wedding last year had been embarrassing. Gia had been walking around telling anyone who would listen that hers and Jay's split was amicable and that they were better off apart. And then she'd been caught with her pants down—well, not really. But when Addi had busted them, Jay's zipper was *open*.

Resting his forehead on hers while her hand worked on him, he blew out a slow breath. "I have to be inside you."

She gripped his face, feeling the stubble on his jaw. His next exhalation brushed over the tender skin on her neck. His desperation matched her own.

"Are you still on birth control?" he asked.

"Yes."

He lifted his head, his blue eyes going stormy gray with lust. With need. With want.

"No condom," she decided, because that was the only decision.

He wasted no time lining up her entrance with the swollen head of his cock, pulling her flush to the edge of the sink. She held his neck, her fingers eagerly bunching his T-shirt while he slid in deeper. *Deeper*.

Seated to the hilt, he blew out a tortured breath that fanned her hair and tickled her ear.

Against that delicate shell, he growled, "God *damn*."

No one had been inside her since he had, and sex in the Mercedes, while that back seat had been a tight fit, had been similar to this time. Out of control with want, they hadn't considered the future.

They hadn't considered the past, either. The years of arguing and misunderstandings. The sadness over their crumbling marriage with each of them helpless to stop it.

Now, though. Ahh, the blessed *now*.

Now was about the physical. About his ability to

turn her on and know what she liked. He displayed that next, by tucking his wide palms around the globes of her ass and pulling her down on top of him. Impaling her while his arms shook with the effort of moving her on and off him. Her breath sawed from her lungs in soft high-pitched sighs.

This was Jayson Cooper at his best.

The first time they'd had sex had been in this very bathroom, in this *very* position. She'd joked then that she was going to marry him "if only to have sex like this on demand whenever I need it."

He must have noticed her mind wandering. He stopped long enough to remind her, "Stay with me. You have an orgasm for me. I know it."

An orgasm for me.

He'd always phrased it that way, as if her having an earth-shattering, bone-rending orgasm was a gift *to him.* Another reason she'd vowed to marry him.

She shut out all other thoughts and concentrated on the sensations in her body. On the soft rub of her nipples on her bra each time he pulled her flush against his chest. On the way he tasted on her tongue, the salt on his skin, the rough scrape of whiskers from where he hadn't shaved yet…

He gripped her hair, balling it in his fist while she explored his neck with her mouth. He loved that.

Scraping her teeth along his jugular, she suckled his earlobe next. "Did Natasha treat you this well, Jay?"

His agonized "no" made her believe that was true.

"Did your skateboarder friend handle you the way I do?"

"Never." She shook her head, feeling naughty that

their dates were still here. Couldn't be helped. Jayson and Gia hadn't been great at avoiding each other even when they'd tried.

They exchanged grins briefly and then they stopped talking. The only sounds were the heated slap of their bodies interspersed with labored breaths until her orgasm rolled over her like a cresting wave, crashing down and taking her mind with it.

For this finite moment, any issues between them were nonexistent. There was only right now—only him coming, the growl in his throat, the stiffening of the muscles in his arms. He filled her, both with his essence and with the deep, guttural moan of completion in her ear.

Eventually, after they'd managed to calm their breathing, he pulled out of her and rested her limp body onto the sink. He braced the sides of the counter, his forehead conking onto her shoulder.

"That—" he said between a deep breath "—was better than the last time we had sex."

In the parking garage. Five days before their divorce.

He wasn't wrong. It *was* better, and on that long-ago day it had been pretty damned incredible.

"When you got it, you got it." She kissed his temple.

He raised his head and his smile nearly took her breath away—as if she needed any help with that. He lowered his mouth to hers for a kiss when the doorknob jiggled.

"Someone in there?" came Addison's voice from the other side of the door.

It occurred to Gia suddenly, alarmingly that she'd

ducked into a bathroom to have sex with her ex at yet another wedding. Only this time, she'd succeeded.

And she'd done it with their dates outside. With the possibility of being caught, she felt more shamed than naughty. She and Jayson had no business carrying on with each other anywhere, let alone *here*, where she might have to explain their behavior to her sister-in-law...

"One second!" she called out then whispered to him, "I can't believe it. Addi's going to bust us *again*."

"Like I said—" He zipped and buttoned his jeans and laid a succinct kiss on her forehead "—some things never change."

Nine

"It's a good thing Royce and Taylor aren't here," Brannon said from the head of the conference room table.

"Agreed," Jayson said. Those two deserved to enjoy their honeymoon and their time together *without* worrying about problems at the office.

"We'll solve the issue before they come home," Gia chimed in from his left. Her eyes flashed quickly from Jayson to Brannon.

As Jayson had expected, she'd been as cool as a cliché cucumber this week. He'd seen her react that way before—after the car sex and the almost-sex last year. She'd let herself go with him, but when they were done, she acted like it'd never happened.

That morning after Royce and Taylor's wedding, Jayson exited the bathroom first with Gia behind him.

Addison had given them a wide-eyed blink followed by a sideways smirk. There was no need to explain. He guessed Addison Abrams had overheard enough to answer any lingering questions she might've had.

Natasha, on the other hand, hadn't noticed he was missing. He'd driven her home, admittedly awkward after their tense date, but she hadn't said much. Though she did make sure and tell him, "It was a nice wedding, but we will not be seeing each other again, Coop."

Fine by him.

He'd called Mason after the drop-off to apologize for potentially ruining his stepbrother's working relationship with Natasha, but Mason assured Jay that his prize supermodel was under contract.

That left Jayson to wonder what the hell he'd been thinking bringing a stranger to a Knox wedding. And further wondering why the hell Gia had done the same thing. But he knew. They'd been trying to fireproof from exactly what had ended up happening anyway.

Jayson couldn't regret it, even if Gia was still giving him the cold shoulder. He, for one, wanted to do it again. No sense in letting perfectly incredible sex rot on the vine.

He wasn't sure where she stood. If she was regretful or reliving the afternoon on a loop in her head the way he was. She was a good actor when she needed to be. And at ThomKnox, under the watching eyes of her brothers, she did some of her best work. He understood why she didn't want to broadcast what happened, but he saw no need in pretending. Addison knew what had happened, so there was a ninety-nine-point-nine percent chance that Brannon knew, too.

He glanced at his ex-wife while her brother pecked at the T13 tablet in his hand. She held Jayson's gaze for an extra beat, licking her top lip before pressing it against her bottom one.

He'd expected an unreadable expression, but hers wasn't unreadable. Her eyes were heated and slightly vulnerable, and the way she jerked her gaze from his gave her away.

She wanted him again. He knew it in his balls. Not such a good actor after all, it seemed.

"I see what you mean." Brannon frowned at the tablet in his hands. "It shuts down."

"That's the bug," Jayson said, his mind returning to the task at hand. The tablet launch last year had been smooth and since then, the sales were above where they'd projected. The software update that was due to go out next month, however, was a hot wad of WTF. "It ran fine last week and now it's not. I have no idea what's transpired since then to screw it up."

Unless Jayson and Gia having sex caused a tear in space and the working part of the software was sucked into a black hole.

Unlikely.

"We'll find the glitch," she reassured all of them, her expression shifting back to calm and collected. "We have the best tech team is the country."

"Damn straight," Jayson agreed. He didn't realize that he and Gia were smiling at each other until Brannon cleared his throat.

"No need to mention this to Taylor or Royce until they're back to work. This issue could go away in a matter of hours." Bran handed the tablet back to Jayson.

Also unlikely. Jayson had complete faith in their tech team, himself included, but he wasn't sure this problem would be resolved that quickly.

"I'll clear my desk and make myself available," Gia said. "You could use the extra brainpower." She smirked at her brother and Jayson and then left the conference room.

"You two seem to be getting along well," Brannon said, his tone droll.

"Yeah." Jayson wasn't giving him any more than that, just in case.

"Guess her and Pip didn't work out."

"Guess not." Jayson smiled.

"How's it going with Natasha?"

"That didn't work out, either. Which I'm assuming you already know."

"It wasn't like you two pulled off a supersecret heist." Bran appeared more amused than angry. "What the hell were you thinking? Your dates were outside having coffee and you and Gia were—" He shook his head.

"My brain wasn't doing any of the thinking."

"I do *not* want to hear details. What Ad told me she heard outside that bathroom door was already too much information." Brannon pushed his hand through his hair.

"Is there an 'if you hurt my baby sister' speech forthcoming?"

"If anyone hurts you," he told Jayson, "it'll be Gia. She's been taking kickboxing, you know."

Jayson frowned. He hadn't known that, actually. He

didn't know a lot about what she did outside of work these days.

"Probably to protect herself from the morons she's contented to date."

"Pip." Bran shook his head. "Why *did* she bring that halfwit to Royce's wedding, anyway?"

"Got me," Jayson said, though he suspected he knew.

"Clock's ticking. Find the mysterious bug that's killing our tablet before Royce returns from his honeymoon," Bran said, obviously glad to change the subject.

"We'll run at it with everything we have. I'll pair everyone up to run code."

"Let me know if you need any monetary support for the venture." Bran slapped Jayson's back as he exited the conference room.

Downstairs, Jayson entered his department and clapped his hands together to get his team's attention. Gia, standing in her office doorway, paused to listen.

"I have a project for you that's going to take precedence over whatever you're currently working on," he announced. The room fell silent as all eyes turned to him. "The good news is I'm paying for overtime and carryout."

"And the bad news?" Gia asked.

"There'll be a lot of both," Jayson answered with a smile.

Jayson stepped into Gia's office and shut the door. He was suited, his jacket in place and his tie knotted.

Each time she'd seen him since last weekend she was reminded of their midnight snack outside, the sexual tension that had been strung so tight she could have played it like a harp. Of course, they both knew where that'd led.

Even though she'd been trying for the last few days to pretend the morning in the bathroom hadn't happened. That she hadn't had sex with the last man on the planet she should've had sex with.

She wrinkled her nose and considered Denver Pippen.

Fine. Jayson was the *second to last* man on the planet she should have sex with.

She'd done a damn good job of keeping her attraction to him in the "There but Unacknowledged" category since they nearly tore each other's clothes off last year. Now she wasn't sure she was hiding it as well.

Shutting her office door behind him, he stalked toward her desk. "I need you."

Because she had sex on the brain, she imagined him throwing her onto her desk and searing her lips with his specific brand of kiss. Instead, he sank into the guest chair.

He crossed his legs ankle-to-knee style and rested one broad palm on his knee. His posture was strong and sure. Nothing new there, but now it served as a reminder that he'd made love to her while standing and supporting her weight using nothing but his arm strength.

"More accurately," he continued. "I need your hardware."

I need your hardware.

"Oh?" she said instead of what she was thinking, which was admittedly half as interesting.

"Big Ben," he answered.

Big Ben was her computer system at home—formerly hers and Jay's home. It had multiple screens, the newest, latest bells and whistles, plus an encrypted cloud back-up system and crazy-fast internet connection set up in the family room. Ben was the Ferrari of home computers. Of course Jay wanted to use it.

"And your software." He tapped his temple with one finger. "I paired everyone off to investigate the bug wreaking havoc on the update. Hell, there could be several bugs for all I know." His eyebrows jumped. "Winner gets a pizza party."

She chuckled. The winner would get more than that—whoever solved this conundrum would attain superhero status.

"If we can fix that bug, it will increase speed and update security on every ThomKnox tablet out there. Our reputation is at stake," he said, serious now.

She felt the same way he did. Despite the casual way he'd asked to borrow her hard- and software, they both knew that ThomKnox's future was nothing to laugh about. Could their company hang with the behemoths, or would ThomKnox forever be second in the technology world?

"Whatever you need," she answered.

"You're the most technically savvy human being in this company." He stood. "Apart from your father."

"And Jack's retired." She used to be shy about flaunting her brains or know-how until she went to college. Leaving for school had given her a freedom she hadn't been able to attain when she'd lived at home. College was the first time she could date without worrying about her father and brothers stating their opinions for the record. As she'd grown up, her family had loosened up, but at times she still felt like a little girl around them.

She'd say this for Jayson: For all his flaws and their incompatibility, he never let her play down her accomplishments. He'd always told her she was smart and to use that to her advantage. *Hell, G, abuse it,* he used to say.

What'd torn them apart ultimately, and a little at a time, was his overprotective nature and need to control every aspect of their shared lives. Now, though, while he was acutely focused on fixing the tablet issue, he didn't seem overbearing at all.

Was she seeing him through sex-colored glasses since their last encounter, or had he really changed?

She shook her head to jar loose that dangerous thought. Jayson had said it himself—they weren't getting back together. And if they weren't getting back together, then there was no reason to wonder if he had changed.

If she kept that front of mind, it would make being alone in the same house alone with him a lot easier. Anything could happen, true, but if they were on the same page, they could solve this issue swiftly and then be done with it. And with each other.

But when he stood and gripped the doorknob to leave, her gaze lingered on his capable hands and strong body.

"I'll bring Thai," he said.

"Okay," she said, even though she wasn't sure it was going to be.

Ten

It'd been a long day.

Gia left her hunchback of Notre Dame posture at the desk in her home office and walked to the sofa to collapse on it.

The square plastic black containers holding the remnants of their Thai dinner were strewn about the coffee table. They'd eaten before and during reviewing the complicated update code but somehow she was hungry again.

She reached for one of the containers and her plastic spoon, slumping back on the couch again. She scooped the tofu green curry on rice and vegetables into her mouth and chewed forlornly.

Jayson joined her, forking a bite of his leftover dinner, Thai Basil Beef, into his mouth. "I don't feel any closer to figuring it out," he said between mouthfuls.

"Me neither. I love lemongrass," she said before her next bite. No sense in talking about their abject failure.

"Someone at work could've had some luck." But they knew better. If any of their team at ThomKnox had found the solution they'd have called Jay immediately. "We'll figure it out."

"Hell yes we will." She set aside her food and straightened her spine. She refused to be felled by one little error. The T13 had been wildly successful and the update would only improve its usage. She wouldn't—couldn't—let her team fail. Er, Jay's team. *Their* team.

The tech department was as close to having kids as they'd come.

"Don't despair." Food container empty, he rested his palm on her knee. Her bare knee thanks to her changing into shorts and a T-shirt. He still wore his pants from work, his sleeves shoved up, his top two buttons open and revealing the bit of dark chest hair she'd always liked. That masculine thatch reminded her that he was capable. And even an independent girl like herself could appreciate his trustworthy side.

Speaking of...

"I owe you for the food. We'll split it." She stood from the couch and walked to her purse, resting on a chair in the corner of the room.

"I got it."

"Jayson. I ate my weight in Thai food tonight."

"So?"

"So, I can pay for my own dinner." She dug some cash from her purse.

"ThomKnox is paying for dinner."

"Well…you picked it up." She waved the bills.

"*No*." He enunciated the word slowly.

"It's important to have boundaries. And this is a good way to establish them."

"Boundaries? The sex on Saturday *established our boundaries*."

"I thought we weren't going to bring that up."

"I thought you would have by now." He walked to where she stood and bracketed her hips with his hands. Before she could lecture herself about kissing him, he'd leaned temptingly close. "Why don't you want to have sex with me?"

She did, but damned if she would admit that. She choked on a laugh and said, "I can think of approximately a million reasons."

But really, there was just one.

Sex with Jayson made her remember being married to him and remembering being married to him made her remember divorcing him and that hurt.

When he lowered his lips to hers each of those million reasons disintegrated into a million pieces. He erased the inch and a half between them and kissed her gently.

She drank in his spicy kiss before she could argue with herself about it. He banded his arms around her waist like he did the last time they were together. When he'd lifted her into his strong arms and held her like she was the only woman on the planet who mattered.

A long time ago, she *was* the only woman who mattered to him. He had taken his duties as husband seriously. Some days too seriously. He'd ruled this house, or had tried anyway. So many of their arguments came from his inability to be flexible on a decision, or his tendency not to include her in the decision at all, and her own insistence that she could take care of herself without him.

Her urge to be independent was a constant refrain she'd grown tired of thinking about. Her whole life she'd been fighting for every inch of independence gained. By the time she was married to Jayson, a man who'd championed her more than any before him, she'd expected to have plenty of that much-needed space.

She pulled her lips from his. How could she expect space from a man who was constantly, and welcomingly, invading hers?

He was breathing heavy, his pupils wide and black. His eyes were her favorite shade of smoky blue. Judging by the state of his pants, he was as turned on as she was.

"We can't," she managed, half expecting him to lean in and prove her wrong.

He didn't.

"You always do this," he said instead. His nostrils flared.

"Do what?" Her blood pressure spiked at his tone, and at losing out on what they both wanted, and she didn't know what he was talking about yet.

"Retreat," he answered. "I don't remember you giving up this easily when we were married."

The reminder that they used to stand in this very room and argue about who knew what was a shadow she couldn't escape.

"Lucky for us we don't have to dig in our heels any

longer, Cooper." She stuffed two twenty-dollar bills, now sweaty in her palm, into his shirt. "Thank you for dinner."

"What the hell did you call me?"

Since he'd just challenged her on retreating, she decided to stay for this battle.

"Everyone calls you Coop or Cooper," she said with a shrug.

His hulking dark presence was less intimidating than it was downright hot. "You're not everyone."

Like a stripper in reverse, he pulled the money from his shirt and dropped it onto the coffee table. "I don't need more reminders that you don't need me, Gia. You've made that perfectly clear."

She was frozen in shock until he turned to leave.

"You are so arrogant!" she called after him. "You only care about getting your way, don't you?"

"Getting my way? You think I'd rather leave than give you an orgasm with this mouth?"

He gestured to his mouth, tempting her since she still felt the imprint of his kiss on her lips. Her knees literally went gooey. Jayson was good with his hands but he was very, very good with his mouth.

"I can take care of myself." But her response was automated. She'd been trying to convince everyone in her life of that for so long, the words came out robotic.

"No, you don't need anyone, do you? Least of all me." His tone was angry, but there was a dose of pain in those words—one she didn't like hearing. Part of her wanted to correct him. To tell him that she'd missed him when they'd split. That his presence in and around the house was what had made this pile of bricks and siding feel like home.

She'd missed him, but she hadn't known how to find her way back to him, either. Not when she'd said so many hurtful things she couldn't take back. She hadn't wanted Jayson's protection and service. She'd wanted to stand as his equal. To experience life with him, not apart from him.

But it was too late for those sorts of observations.

Their standoff lasted several seconds. He stood, silently daring her to give in to her wants—her *need*. But they'd already given in to the temptation and sex hadn't solved anything. Worse, their at-work conversations had been laced with hidden innuendo. Her mind wasn't on her work, it was in his pants. And as long as that was the case, they'd never fix this damned update.

"We have an important job to do," she said, leaning on her old friend, Pragmatism. "We shouldn't let ourselves be distracted."

"Yeah," was all he said before he gathered his bag and walked out of the room. She stood and listened to him go, closing her eyes against the finality of the front door quietly shutting.

Eleven

"I should let you two rest."

Jayson meant to hand back Addison and Brannon's daughter right away, but he delayed. Quinn Marie Knox was nestled in his arms and cooing up at him. A series of gurgles and grunts came from the precious bundle, her big eyes taking in as much of the world around her as they could. Tiny fingers clutched and released the air and he was fairly certain he'd lost his heart to her.

Finally, he was able to release baby Quinn in her mother's arms. "Sorry it took me so long to stop by."

Addison had gone into labor the night he and Gia had eaten Thai food and argued. The same night he'd kissed her and had hoped to end up in her bed, or hell, at least on the couch.

But, no.

In spite of the desire surging within and between them, Gia had retreated. Once again he'd found himself surrounding her with the protection and love he thought she needed, only to watch her retreat.

He stepped in, she stepped back. The dance continued. He wondered if he'd ever learn.

Addison adjusted her baby girl against her chest, who was nuzzling to be breastfed. "That's okay, Coop. I know you're busy."

"Say bye to Uncle Jayson." She waved her daughter's closed fist.

He smiled and waved back. Uncle Jayson. He liked that.

Family had always been important to him. Losing his marriage with Gia had been the ultimate failure. He didn't know what he would've done if he lost his work and his in-laws, too. The Knoxes stitched everyone into their family quilt—and once you were there, you didn't want to leave.

Jayson exited the sitting room and wandered through the kitchen. Bran was at the back door, pulling on a pair of boxing gloves. Once they were on, he punched them together. "Ready?"

"As I'll ever be." Jayson hadn't been through training Bran had, but he knew how to scrap. *Without* gloves. He'd gone a round or two with his own father and had lost. Badly. At age twelve he'd stepped between his abusive father and his mother, and had taken hits for her. He'd never been prouder of a black eye in his life.

Since then he'd developed a penchant for protecting those he loved, made easier when his mother remarried a good man and in turn gave Jayson a brother. He smiled as he considered Bran's and Addi's daughter. That little girl would never have to wonder if she was loved or safe a day in her life.

"She's great, your daughter," he told Bran.

"Those Knox genes." Bran grinned. "Although she inherited all the beauty from my wife."

Not all of it. Jayson found himself thinking of Gia. Again.

After stepping into the ring and receiving some basic instruction, Jayson was throwing punches comfortably at his ex-brother-in-law. Bran's backyard was lush with green grass and flowers and trees. It was a strange setup for trying to kick the other man's ass.

Not that there was any animosity lingering between them. Throwing punches at the middle Knox sibling was more about technique than working through a problem.

Jayson was frustrated with the way things *hadn't* gone with Gia, but there was no need for him to exercise that frustration physically. He preferred to funnel that irritation into his work—namely solving the problem with the tablet before Royce and Taylor arrived home from their honeymoon.

Jayson finally landed a hit on Bran's ribs and earned a satisfying grunt from his opponent. Bran caught his breath against the ropes, nodding that he was done.

"You're a fast learner," he praised as he and Jayson stepped from the ring.

A pair of loungers was set up in the grass, a cooler of ice-cold beer bottles between them.

"And I thought your daughter was beautiful. That

cooler is a sight." Jayson accepted a beer and sat down, spinning off the cap and taking a long, refreshing slug.

Bran let out a beer commercial–worthy "Ahhhh."

After Bran reminded Jayson to keep his face protected in the ring, he paused, stared into his beer bottle and asked, "You and Gia avoiding each other?"

Here we go.

"Why?"

"You two arrive separately to meetings. I thought at first you were trying to make it look like you weren't dating by avoiding each other, but since Quinn was born, it seems like things went south."

"Well. Well. Look who's become observant."

"Very funny."

"I was being serious." This was the same man who, last year, hadn't had a single clue that Addison was madly in love with him. If it hadn't been for Bran and Addi's road trip to Lake Tahoe, Jayson wondered if Bran would have ever figured it out.

"So am I," Bran said, studying Jayson closely. "What's going on? Gia and Addi were talking when Gia was here yesterday, but Addi told me she's sworn to secrecy." Bran took a swig from his bottle. "Can you believe that?"

"Yeah, I believe it." Jayson sighed. "Nothing happened. Not really. We worked. She insisted on paying me for her half of dinner. We fell into old patterns of arguing like we did when we were married." He shrugged, unsure how else to explain it to someone who had been married for about two minutes. "It's hard after a while. The arguments become tiresome. And they're never about what they're about."

"Meaning Gia's paying for dinner was about more than money." Bran, his gaze unfocused on the yard, shook his head. "She always wanted to be treated like one of the guys. I suspect it's because of having two older brothers. And of course, we have this adorable kid sister who is a smart-ass, but loves so fiercely it's undeniable. All we wanted to do was protect her from anything—or anyone—that might make her cry."

Jayson stared at Bran's profile in deep thought. He could relate to that. How many times had he stepped in to protect Gia the way he'd stepped in to protect his mother? Only Gia hadn't really needed that sort of protection. There was no dragon to slay where his ex-wife was concerned.

But for the first time he considered how Bran and Royce, and Jack, too, had handled Gia with kid gloves. She wouldn't have seen their efforts as protection, but as them stunting her growth. She'd wanted to flourish on her own, without their involvement.

And, he reasoned, without his as well.

"She's not weak," Jayson said, and wondered if his protectiveness made her feel like he thought she was. Then he remembered a bunch of other arguments that had ended with her accusing him of being "controlling" and he didn't have to wonder any longer.

"I overstepped," Jayson admitted for the first time in his life.

"By buying her dinner?" Bran asked, dubious.

"In the past. By telling her what she needs. By making decisions without her. By refusing to let her stand on her own two feet."

"You were trying to take care of her. We all saw

that." Bran sipped his beer. "Plus you know how much she loves to win. She'll do anything to make you see her point of view."

"She stuffed the money down my shirt."

"'Course she did," Bran laughed. "Listen, whatever stuff you and G have going on is your business. I care about you both, but I also know you're capable of working things out. I just wanted to make sure I wasn't going to lose the dream team when it came to fixing this tablet issue."

"Gia and I are pros at dancing around each other," Jayson assured his friend.

That was the truth. They knew how to button down and focus on work. No matter what had happened between them since their divorce, they would prioritize ThomKnox and fix the tablet because nothing was more important than that.

Almost nothing… but there was no fixing what had been broken between him and Gia.

Twelve

The motivation to succeed was an attribute Jayson and Gia shared. Which was why they'd agreed that on Saturday, he'd return to the house and fire up Big Ben, and the three of them would make a decent bit of headway.

He'd been working for four hours straight without coming up for air when Gia interrupted.

"How's it going?" She was carrying her own T13 while his was being used as a coaster for his coffee cup. Without a solution for the update, "coaster" was the only purpose the tablet would serve. She moved the empty mug, clucking her tongue.

She didn't need to say anything. That small gesture spoke volumes.

It spoke of mini arguments about using a coaster or a napkin, about not resting his shoes on the coffee table. All insignificant, but they had a way of becoming bigger and bigger over time—the way individual grains of sand eventually became an island.

That's what he and Gia had between them. An island of misunderstandings and assumptions.

"I thought I had a breakthrough, but it turned out to be nothing." He might as well be talking about them. He'd had an inkling of the part he'd played in the deterioration of their marriage, but hell if he knew what to do about it now.

She seemed content to keep her distance. She'd worked by the pool today rather than inside the house, and when she did venture into the house, she grabbed whatever was fastest to eat before returning to the pool again.

"We'll find it." She sounded tired, as if she might not believe that.

He understood how hard it was to admit something was unfixable. Admitting as much about their marriage had been the most difficult thing he'd ever done.

"I'm going to run a few errands. I can't look at a screen any longer." She started to leave the room but he wasn't ready to let her go yet. In an attempt to keep her attention, he dealt a low blow.

"Finally met our niece," he said, receiving the smile he'd expected.

She crossed her arms over a simple sundress that looked anything but simple on his ex-wife. Her curves tantalizingly stretched every seam.

"I love that both Addison and Taylor have baby girls. Serves my male-dominated family right."

Remembering what Bran had told him, Jayson said, "They were overprotective."

"Men tend to treat me like fine china."

"Not a bad thing to be cared for." He still didn't fully understand why she didn't like her family looking out for her. He'd have given anything for a father who wanted to protect him at all costs.

"I had to run off to MIT for my brothers to admit I grew up. Jack didn't catch on ever, I don't think."

Yeah. Jayson didn't think so, either. Gia's father had stepped in time and again to make sure she was taken care of. Including with her husband. Whenever he thought of Jack's conversation with him before he and Gia married, Jayson bristled. Mistakes were definitely made.

"I'm not fragile," she stated now, and just stubbornly as she had in the past. "And I don't give up. On anything."

He thought of something else he and Bran talked about—how competitive she was, and suddenly had a great idea.

"Except you're going shopping. So you sort of are giving up."

She made a disgusted sound. "I'm taking a break. Breaks are good for the brain."

So was sex.

"I'll bet you I find and fix the bug before you do." She was smart, but so was he. "We've been stuck on this for far too long. Maybe what we need is a little friendly competition to motivate us."

"I'm plenty motivated." But her eyebrow arched

high on her forehead, a sure sign she'd been properly provoked. "I know I'll find the problem before you do."

"If you're so sure, then why not bet?" he goaded.

"What do you have that I could possibly want?"

When he held out his arms, she rolled her eyes, but her smile was worth it. "Be serious."

"Okay." He thought for a second, and then landed on the one offer she couldn't refuse. "If you win, I'll cook for you."

She snorted.

"My grandmother's homemade pasta."

Her mouth dropped open.

He grinned, knowing he had her. He didn't make his grandmother's homemade pasta recipe often, but he had made it for Gia when they were married—for their anniversaries. Both of them.

"I can guess what you want if you win." She folded her arms. "I'm not having sex with you again."

"You're sure you'll win. What are you worried about?"

"Hmm. Well I *was* sure. You're pretty motivated by sex." Her smile held. She didn't hate this idea. Not even a little.

"I admit, that's a good motivator." Especially sex with her. "But this time we're not doing it on a bathroom counter. We'll be in bed."

He tipped his head and walked closer, daring her to say no. To admit that she was afraid of losing, and therefore sleeping with him. Or worse, to refuse the bet because she didn't *want* to sleep with him.

She did neither.

Because she'd sooner die than admit she didn't think

she could win. Plus, as he'd suspected, she wanted to sleep with him again.

She folded her arms over her breasts. "This is bribery. I love that pasta more than anything."

"I know." He loved every second of this exchange. He slid by her and headed for the kitchen. "Have fun shopping. I'll be here toiling away on a solution."

"Shopping can wait," she said. "If I'm going to win, I may as well do it. Also, I expect the works for my meal. Candles. Music. I want to walk in and mistake my kitchen for a fancy Italian restaurant."

Yep. He had her. Now all he had to do was win.

"Sounds like you're taking the bet." He pulled open the refrigerator and pretended to search for something to eat.

"Okay, Jay." She faced him. "We have a deal."

She picked up her tablet and walked through the kitchen, sliding her sunglasses onto her nose. She took her place outside on the lounger by the pool.

The clock was officially ticking. He no longer cared whether or not he found the problem before Royce and Taylor came home.

All he had to do was find it before Gia did.

Gia justified her decision not to shop since she had something to wear to her date tomorrow. Nothing new, but still.

She'd spent the remainder of the day hunched over her notes and her tablet, though sadly didn't feel much closer to the answer than before.

The stakes were high. Jayson's grandmother's pasta recipe was nothing to joke about. Plus, while sex with him was off the charts fantastic, she also knew the repercussions of falling into bed with him again.

She didn't need to feel any more for him than she already did. Letting her heart be involved after she'd put their marriage *and* divorce to bed could be disastrous. She was supposed to be moving on, but here she was a year and a half later and not only had she had sex with him already, he was inside their former shared house right now.

Which was why she didn't cancel her date.

She'd paused from her work by the pool to check her messages on the Divinely Yours app. She had several, including one from Denver Pippen. He mentioned he'd be out of the country for a skateboarding competition in Germany. He let her down easy, telling her know that while he'd had fun at the wedding, he didn't see them going further.

She agreed, but appreciated his candor. He could've ghosted her, but chose to lay out the facts. Pip wasn't a bad guy, he just wasn't right for her.

She'd scrolled down through a few seriously gross offers in her inbox before coming across a message from a name she recognized. Elias Hill.

Elias was the founder/owner of Hill Yacht Company. He'd praised her work at ThomKnox and then invited her out on the maiden voyage of his latest model before it hit the showroom floor. He'd sealed the deal at the end: "No pressure, Gia. Just a day on the water."

She *so* needed a day without pressure.

She didn't expect a relationship to bloom from a yacht-date with Elias Hill. But if the unthinkable happened and Jayson won this bet, she could lean on the excuse of dating Elias and avoid going to bed with Jayson. That was cheating, she supposed, but didn't they say that all was fair in love and war?

Yawning, she gathered her things and headed inside. She was done for today and looking forward to curling up with a cup of tea and a good book. It was time for Jayson to head home, too. He'd been tireless, but he had to give up at some point.

Plus, she needed to tell him about the date—which he wouldn't like—and let him know that the house was off-limits while she was away. They could resume their investigation on Monday when they were both working.

But halfway through those thoughts, she found her ex-husband, the heels of his sneakers resting on the arm of the sofa, fast asleep.

"Jayson." A familiar frustration bubbled up at the sight of him sprawled out, his shoes on the furniture. Irritation was easy to come by when she spotted his empty coffee cup and a plate with crumbs on it left on the table.

And yet, she didn't have the heart to wake him. He had to be exhausted. He'd admitted earlier today that he hadn't slept well this week, too worried about this update fix. There was something so vulnerable about the way his long eyelashes shadowed his cheeks. And something so animal about the way his dark scruff decorated his jaw. She remembered the last time he'd kissed her, his whiskers abrading her chin. How hard it'd been to stop kissing him. To put up her guard and turn him down when her body had begged her to continue…

She tossed a blanket over him rather than wake him,

reassured that the date tomorrow was exactly what she needed. There was a time when she would've kissed the corner of Jayson's mouth and told him it was time for bed. A time when he would've pulled her down into his arms and said, "Lie with me a while."

No longer.

Their passion and sexual need for each other was alive and well, but their ability to be vulnerable had vanished. She mourned that briefly as she flipped off the lamp. But by the time she locked the front and back doors and headed upstairs to bed, she justified that her mourning period was well and truly over.

Already she could feel herself softening toward her ex-husband, those old feelings lurking around in her head and, if she wasn't careful, in her heart.

That was one risk she wasn't willing to take.

Thirteen

Jayson exited the downstairs bathroom and wandered into the kitchen. He'd fallen asleep in his former house. Being here this early in the morning, and stumbling into the kitchen in search of coffee, was so familiar it was bizarre.

He didn't know if he was more surprised he'd slept through the night or that Gia had let him stay.

He could hear her moving around upstairs, but evidently she'd been in here earlier. Coffee was made, most of the pot gone. He poured what was left into a mug and took a long draw.

"Morning." Gia breezed into the kitchen dressed in a bright pair of shorts and a shimmery shirt. Her shoes were tall. Her toenails painted the same color pink as her shorts.

"You look nice," he said, unable to keep from running his eyes over those tanned, smooth legs. Her hair was wavy and draped over her shoulders, the way he liked it.

"Thanks," she replied.

"I'm making more coffee," he told her as she gathered her purse and stuck a pair of sunglasses on top of her head. "Sorry I crashed on the couch. I was beat."

"No big deal." She flashed him a quick smile.

"Where are you off to?" Apparently, he was going to have to ask.

"Oh, I have a thing." She waved a hand like she wasn't going to say more but then she did. "A date."

"A date." What the hell?

"Yes. It's a casual day on a yacht."

"With who?"

"Jayson. This isn't any of your business."

He knew that. He forced a smile, hoping it'd gain him an inch. "Just curious if you and Pip ended up working everything out."

"No." She said it with enough finality that he believed her. "I met today's date on the same app where I met Denver, though. His name is Elias Hill."

"You're still on the dating app?" He blinked down at his coffee, wondering if he was still asleep. Or hallucinating. After what had happened between them at the wedding, he hadn't expected her to be *dating*.

She started for the front door and he chased after her, careful not to spill his coffee. "Is that safe?"

"Is what safe?" she asked, grabbing her keys.

"Going on a boat with a guy who could be a serial killer."

"Jay." She gave him a bland look. "Elias Hill is the CEO of a billion-dollar yacht company. I doubt he has murder on the high seas at the front of his mind."

Jealousy roared to life inside him at the same time he had the realization that even though this setup felt familiar—them waking up in the same house and chatting over coffee—there was one big difference.

They were no longer married.

If she wanted to go on a date, she could. Still, he couldn't help saying, "I don't like it."

"You don't have to." She patted his cheek with one hand.

Then she was out the door, leaving him in need of a shower, a second cup of coffee and an excuse to stick around. Any good friend would make sure she returned home safely from her date.

Elias Hill had been perfectly nice. Perfectly casual. Perfectly polite and perfectly suited for someone like her. He liked talking business but knew when to relax. He didn't have any dumb come-on lines and he didn't call her "baby" or "Jee-ahh" the way Denver Pippen had.

Elias was…well, perfect.

He was also perfectly *boring*.

By the time they'd had lunch, she was yawning behind her hand. She tried to convince herself it was because she'd stayed up late working. Because she'd had trouble sleeping knowing her ex-husband was downstairs—the man was majorly throwing off her chi. But all that line of thinking did was bring Jayson back to the forefront of her thoughts and then she'd ended up comparing him to Elias.

Elias's muscles beneath his white shirt looked nice enough, but he somehow lacked the roundness through the shoulders that Jayson had. His forearms were fine, but she doubted he had the strength to lift her up so she could wrap her ankles at his waist. His face was pleasant, but too clean-cut. His lips were too narrow. His hair, wavy in the breeze, was thinner than Jay's full, thick, but short locks.

Elias was as boring as his stale, white outfit—a literal blank slate—and his personality barely appeared. He spoke carefully and evenly, but his stories droned on, and the last one about the investors' party meandered and looped but in the end had no point.

He wasn't witty. He wasn't stubborn. He wasn't challenging.

He isn't Jayson, her mind offered and she told it promptly to shut up.

She didn't want Jayson. That was her mantra after they docked, after she'd allowed Elias to kiss her cheek and as she drove home. So intent on making that her new truth, she decided that working side by side with Jayson was probably a bad idea. Bet or no bet, she needed to put some distance between them.

When she stepped into the kitchen of her house and looked out the window, instead of finding peace in being alone she found Jayson Cooper in her pool.

He was naked save for a pair of board shorts, and floating on a yellow raft shaped like a lemon slice. He should have looked ridiculous, especially wearing a pair of pink sunglasses that belonged to her, but he didn't.

He looked damned tempting with a solid tan and a five o'clock shadow darkening his jaw. He was cradling a can of sparkling water in one hand, his head leaning back, showcasing the column of his strong neck. Beads of water danced along his body, glistening in the waning sun.

Her mouth watered.

How dare her body react to him? He ruined everything—including her date. If not for sleeping with Jayson so recently, she might have found Elias Hill perfectly pleasant.

Perfect. *Yuck.*

She replayed that dumb story about the family dog he'd told her and cringed. How was it that a billionaire yacht CEO wasn't more interesting?

"What the hell are you doing here?" she growled, tossing her beach bag onto an empty lounger. She was still wearing her new bikini beneath her shorts and top and had been planning on coming home and swimming off her frustration.

"You're back. Didn't expect you for a while." He finished off his water and crunched the can with one hand before tossing it to the side of the pool. "I was going to leave, but I was caught up in working and decided to take a dip. I was planning to be gone by the time you came home."

"Sure you were." But him being here didn't piss her off as much as she wanted it to.

Especially when concern leaked into his tone when he asked, "Didn't go well?"

She crossed her arms and shrugged.

A frown bisected his eyebrows. "What the hell did that bastard do?"

She dropped her arms. "Nothing. I'm not mad about my date. I'm mad because you're here and I want to swim."

"I have to leave so you can swim?" When he said it out loud it did sound silly.

"Whatever. It's hot and I'm frustrated and I'm coming in."

Hands in her hair, she pulled her waves into a ponytail and stripped out of her clothes. She was aware of Jayson watching her from behind those pink sunglasses. Especially since this bikini was gorgeous. The hot pink suit covered what it needed to, but the peekaboo mesh at the neckline hinted at what she was hiding.

She stepped to the zero-entry side and started down the ramp, the warm water lapping at her ankles, then calves, then knees. She commented about how the water was colder than she'd expected and he grinned.

"Don't." She warned, sealing her fate.

He was off the raft in a shot, tossing the sunglasses to the side of the pool and then…he was gone.

"I just washed my hair!" she shouted as he cut through the water. Before she could turn to walk up the ramp, he'd surfaced and scooped her into his arms like Swamp Thing.

"You know better than to tell me the water's cold, G," he said, his eyelids lowering ominously.

She kicked her legs uselessly and wiggled in his grip. "I take it back!" she said through breathless laughter.

"You can't take it back." He laid a hard kiss on her mouth and walked her toward the deep end. Before she could beg him not to throw her in, he'd already tossed her into the air.

Fourteen

What was more fun? Kissing and then throwing Gia into the deep end or watching her try and catch him while he swam left then right in a zigzag?

Kissing her, definitely. With or without the throwing. Though throwing her in had been fun, and something he'd done time and time again after they'd bought this house.

"Dammit, Jay!" she sputtered after she surfaced.

"You know better than to step into the water with me. You'll end up wet." Letting the double entendre hang, he gave her a wicked smile and added, "In *or* out of the water."

"You're an ass." She launched herself at him but this time he didn't move, catching her instead. He wrapped her legs around his waist and walked her into deeper water.

"I have a very nice ass. Or so I've been told."

She rolled her eyes. "Is that what *Natasha* told you?"

"Natasha didn't think of anyone but herself most of the time. Care to share about Elias?"

She pouted, but didn't move to escape his grip. "No comment."

"Were you trying to make me jealous by going on a date?"

"I was trying to take my mind off of you!" She jerked her gaze away like she hadn't meant to admit that.

"Oh, really." He gave her a squeeze. "Did it work?"

She tightened her arms around his neck. In this position every one of her curves lined up with his body perfectly. What he wouldn't give to have a taste of her mouth, or feel her ride him, those thighs locked tight…

"I'm not seeing Elias again."

That was evasive, but some damn good news.

"Why'd you go out with him in the first place?"

"Because sleeping with you is a really, really bad idea."

"Ouch." That hurt.

The divorce had been hard on both of them—he knew that. But he'd also figured out that they hadn't had their fill of each other yet. A marriage was more than attraction, but that didn't mean they couldn't have fun together while in each other's immediate proximity.

"You already slept with me."

She sighed. "I know. I don't think we should do it again."

He felt the corners of his mouth pull down. "Why the hell not?"

"How's this going to work, Jay? We give in to our physical attraction, and then what? Walk away?"

That was the gist. But she sounded as wounded as he felt at the idea.

"What's the alternative? You've made it clear you don't want me in your space permanently."

"That's not fair."

"No, but it's true."

She quirked her lips, and he guessed it was because he'd made a good point.

"We tried to repair our marriage and work together. We failed. I'm not sure much has changed since then."

They were the same people, he couldn't argue that. "Yes, but we know what it costs to be together. We know better than make the same mistakes we made before. That has to count for something."

She watched him and he watched her. The water lapped against his waist and her thighs, which were still cradled in his hands.

"Gia. If you don't want—"

She kissed him and cut off the offer he hadn't wanted to make. He'd been about to reassure her that if she didn't want to sleep with him, she didn't have to—bet or no bet.

Turned out she put his tongue to better use. Her mouth moved on his. Softly. *Slowly.* This was nothing like the day in her parents' vacation house kitchen—or the bathroom interlude that followed. They explored each other carefully, like neither of them wanted to spook the other away.

Her hand vanished into the water and next he felt her tender grip on his erection.

He grunted, hardly able to breathe now that she was handling him with long, even strokes. She smoothed her lips over his open mouth, tempting him, turning him on so much his brain wasn't operating at full capacity.

But he couldn't keep from replaying her words— and the wave of regret they'd arrived on.

He ended the kiss and looked his ex-wife in the eyes. "I don't want to fail with you again, G."

Damn. That was honest. More honest than he'd meant to be.

She released him, untwined her legs from his hips and swam for the ladder. He thought that was it, that she'd changed her mind and, hell, maybe that was for the better. For them to cut their losses and let go of the idea of *them* altogether.

But then she turned and looked over her shoulder before climbing out and said, "Well. Come on."

He followed obediently, his eyes feasting on the vision of his ex-wife climbing the ladder. She pulled herself from the water, her long, soaking hair arrowing down her back, a trickle of water flowing over her tanned skin. Her plush bottom in that hot pink bikini. God, he could take a bite out of her—she looked that damn delicious.

Even if this was a bad idea, he wasn't as future focused as Gia. He didn't give a damn what happened in a day or a week or a month from now. Whenever he was with her physically, the world was suddenly right.

Everything made sense for the time they were together and that was enough for him.

She toweled off and he did the same, quickly. Unlike his apartment where everyone could see everyone, they didn't have to worry about privacy in this backyard.

The house was in a neighborhood but not the tightly packed suburbia that he'd grown up in. Here, the houses were spaced out enough that no one could peer over at them from an upstairs window. That fact, and the tall white privacy fence around the entire backyard, was probably why Gia let him take off her bikini top.

He released her gorgeous breasts into his hands, stroking the chilled buds. The sun was receding fast, the cooler air blowing in, but he didn't want to suggest they go inside. He was afraid she'd have second thoughts. They had momentum, and if they lost it, they might never find it again.

She shivered as she slipped her bikini bottoms off her legs. He followed suit, kicking off his shorts in record time. Then he stared.

He loved Gia's body. He always had. And now he was going to love her body from head to toe—for as long as she could stand it.

She'd always loved foreplay and he'd been more than willing to take his time with her. They hadn't had the chance for foreplay the last time they were together. He intended on remedying that.

He backed her to the rattan chaise lounger and laid her down. "Are you—"

She hushed him with her finger against his lips. Clearly she didn't want to give herself a chance to have second thoughts either. She ran that same finger down his chest, belly button and lower as she sat on the lounger.

When she navigated his favorite part of his body into her mouth, whatever thoughts had been bouncing around in his head vanished. There was only the feel of her heated mouth suctioned onto him.

He rested his hand on the back of her head while she worked, admiring her grace and beauty while she took him on her tongue. She was the best. He hadn't been a saint while they were divorced, so he knew of what he spoke.

Gia blew his mind. Thoroughly. She didn't try to impress him; she simply enjoyed herself. Pleased with herself for pleasing him. So focused on him, she must not have noticed when he gently cupped her jaw to stop her. She took him to the hilt again, one long, slick slide that had him welding his molars together.

He forced himself from her mouth, bending at the waist while he waited for the spots to clear from his vision. He wanted to finish inside her tonight.

She peered up at him, eyes wide. When she licked the corner of her mouth, he worried he might come right then. He was a grown man, in charge of his faculties most of the time, but this was his weak point.

She was his weak point. His ultimate Achilles heel.

He was starting to see what she meant about this being a bad idea, but damned if he'd stop now. He tossed his beach towel on the concrete and lowered to his own knees in front of the lounger.

Pushing her shoulders, he encouraged her to lie back. He didn't have to convince her much. Propped up, arms draped over her head, she was a goddess.

The purple-pink sky intensified the surreal moment, the water droplets still clinging to her skin sparkling in the fading light.

He bent and licked a drop off her nipple, then the side of her breast. He repeated the action on the other side, not wanting to give one breast an unfair amount of attention. Then he ran his tongue down her middle to her belly button while her hands sank into his hair and gave a little tug.

"Someone's excited," he murmured against her damp flesh.

"It's been a while," she breathed.

He liked hearing that way too much.

"I'll be down here awhile to make up for it."

Promise made, he tugged her so she was flat on her back, and then rested her knees on his shoulders. Her open before him was a gift. She trusted him with her pleasure. It hadn't been enough to save their marriage, but he was proud she was willing to give herself to him.

He kissed the insides of her knees and worked higher and higher up her thigh. Her breaths tightened, and he drank in her anticipation. It gave him strength to know that she needed this—not only the orgasm, but an orgasm that only he could deliver.

Wedging a space for his shoulders, he dipped his head and tasted her, dragging his tongue in one slow line.

She shivered.

He did it again, this time flattening his tongue.

She shuddered.

With a proud smile to himself, he renewed his efforts and dove in, this time not letting up until her cries of completion were echoing across the nighttime sky.

Fifteen

Julia and Albert Robinson's patio was a work of art. The built-in stone grill sat in the center, the matching tiled bar top wrapping around each side. It took up at least half the space available, the other half filled with an oversize square outdoor dining table and eight chairs. Overkill for their modest house, but his mom wouldn't let Jayson buy her a house. He had to be happy with what they'd accept—in this case a brand new back patio design for her for a Mother's Day gift. Next year he'd talk her into an in-ground pool.

His mother deserved to be spoiled, though he would admit his stepdad did a good job of spoiling her in all the ways he could. Albert had padded their retirement fund, made sure she felt safe and loved. But Albert couldn't afford the extras that Jayson could provide.

Jay made a hell of a lot of money and without a family of his own to support, figured he could afford to spoil them.

The glass patio door slid open and Chester, Mason's husband, stepped outside with a tray of burgers and brats, the vegetarian versions for himself. "Mas, hon, bring me a beer," he called over his shoulder.

"Can I help?" Jayson held out a hand.

"Yes, occupy your brother so he doesn't get in my way," Chester said with a good-natured eye roll.

While Chester and Albert decided what grill arrangement was optimum for the burgers and brats, being careful not to "contaminate" Chester's veggie fare, Mason and Jayson sat at the far side of the newly built bar. Their mother was inside finishing up her famous deviled potato salad.

"I like this dining set," Mason said before sipping his beer.

"Glad they let me do it."

"You're a good son. If you're trying to win, you've done it."

Jayson knew his brother was kidding. Mason was driven, ambitious—one didn't accidentally become a standout photographer in the fashion industry—but he was also laid-back. When the topic of conversation rounded to Natasha, Jayson shook his head.

"I should have warned you," Mason said. "She's a diva. Gorgeous, but a diva."

"Gia's prettier," Jayson muttered.

Mason's silence was deafening. He smirked. "What is going on?"

"Nothing's going on. It was just an observation." Jay took a swig of his own beer.

"I noticed you were in a better mood than usual and I couldn't figure out why. Now I know. Sex with the ex."

"Don't be crass," Chester called out before addressing Jayson. "I would love it if you two found your way back to each other."

"He's a romantic," Mason chided.

"Romance is a tall order for Gia and me," Jayson said, meaning it. They'd tried the happily-ever-after route, went off-road and ended up in a ditch.

He considered Albert, and his mother who joined him at the grill, and Mason and Chester. Maybe romance wasn't a tall order for his family, but it seemed an insurmountable leap for Jayson.

"I'm going to check the garden." Jayson stood abruptly and left his family on the patio. He stepped around the side yard to where his mother kept a small herb garden. Over the fence, the neighbor's squatty bulldog barked hello.

"Hey, Ollie." He grinned down at the portly dog who wagged the entire back half of his body since his nub of a tail was incapable of the action. Jayson bent over the top half of the fence and gave Ollie a scratch before settling on the stone bench next to the garden.

He'd always wanted this sort of peace for his mother. This house, this neighborhood was a huge step up from where he'd grown up with a father who made their lives a living hell for far too long.

Only a boy at the time, Jayson had vowed to save his mom from the adult man who wasn't man enough to pick on someone his own size. Thankfully his mother had friends. The first—and only—time Eric Cooper had hit Jayson in the face, she'd left with Jayson in tow and had run straight to those friends.

By the time they'd returned home two days later, Eric was gone. Julia changed the locks and began looking for a new apartment immediately—even before the house was listed on the market.

She'd picked up a second job, and then a third, and Jayson grew up fending for himself. He'd seen his role as the protector, until Albert stepped into their lives and took over. Albert, a nerdy type who at first didn't seem capable of slaying a butterfly let alone a dragon, had been adamant about their boys being kids and not worrying about adult problems. He assigned household duties, relegating Jayson to trash duty and Mason to lawn mowing.

Jayson grew up the rest of the way like a normal kid, and would be forever grateful to Albert for giving him a good childhood. He hadn't known at the time that Albert was saving him, though. There'd been moments where he'd argued and yelled, but Albert seemed to understand that Jayson had been raised by a man with no boundaries. Boundaries that Albert set gently, but firmly.

Once grown, Jayson was determined to provide his mother and stepfather with the sorts of things they'd done without on their quest of raising two teenagers— one of them angry thanks in part to DNA and past trauma, the other struggling with his sexuality.

Jayson had been lucky. Some kids didn't make it out of a dark past as cleanly.

When he'd met Gia, his world had stopped. Honest to God, it'd been like a movie. He'd spotted her across the room, the soundtrack of a cheesy ballad playing in the background.

When he'd gone to her father to ask for his daughter's hand in marriage, Jack replied, "As long as you take care of her." Jack had gone on to explain that he knew he couldn't always be there for his daughter, and now that was Jayson's duty.

Jayson had taken that duty seriously. He knew how to take care of a woman, knew what she needed.

Or so he thought.

Each time he tried to do his *husbandly duty*, Gia had shut him down. Now that they were divorced she needed him less than ever.

In his efforts to be a good man, a good husband and nothing like his father, had he gone about being a husband the wrong way? He'd never laid a hand on Gia—he'd sooner die—but he'd strong-armed her in other ways, hadn't he? He'd tried corralling her the way Jack had—protecting her the way Royce and Bran had. And like she'd done with each of those other men, she'd pulled away from Jayson, too.

Flubbing a marriage was a big failure for him. He'd never intended on divorcing. He'd planned on being married one time, for forever. But as their communication deteriorated, he found himself swallowing arguments instead of having them. He'd opted for silence over involvement. He should have told her what he was thinking. What he was *feeling*.

At the time he hadn't wanted to be wrong.

Stupid.

"You two aren't related, but you're a lot alike." Chester appeared around the corner, gave Ollie the bulldog a scratch on the head and then sat next to Jayson. "I have a thing for the strong, silent type. I can't help it. If you need to talk, I'm a good listener."

Jayson debated before giving in. He could use a second opinion on the thoughts ricocheting off the inside of his skull.

"Gia and I have a complicated past, but I think a future would be even more complicated."

"Possibly. It's hard not to go back to that familiarity, though. Been there. My ex before Mason." Chester shook his head. "It didn't end well, but we weren't anything like you and Gia."

Jayson turned his head. "Meaning?"

"You two are good for each other, but you're each holding on to your pride with both hands. Vulnerability is the key to any good relationship."

"Gia and I have been naked together, Ches. *Recently.* How much more vulnerable can you get?"

Chester patted Jayson's shoulder. "Jayson, Jayson. Sometime you should try admitting you made a mistake. That goes a long way."

"She's the one pushing me away." Jayson stood. It hurt to admit that out loud. He assumed that hurt was the vulnerability Ches had been referring to.

"I'll stay out of it," Chester vowed as he stood, also. "After I say one more thing."

Jayson could have guessed his brother-in-law wouldn't keep completely silent.

"Even if you don't ride off into the sunset together,

if spending time together helps you and Gia over a hump—no pun intended—then go for it."

"That doesn't exactly sound like you," Jayson narrowed his eyes in suspicion. "I thought you were rooting for us to get back together."

"Always." Chester smoothed a finger over one manicured eyebrow. "I also recognize that you are happier when you're talking about her, and I like seeing you happy. Don't beat yourself up so much about the past. These things have a way of working themselves out."

He patted Jayson's leg and then walked off.

Jayson stood for a solid minute and watched a honeybee visit flower after flower at the edge of his mother's garden.

He *was* happier with Gia in his life. He couldn't argue that. He was happier sleeping with her, too. He thought about her happiness, then and wondered…

Had he prioritized his own happiness over hers in the past? Had she been telling him what she needed this whole time but he hadn't listened?

Ollie barked, interrupting his thoughts.

"Yeah, yeah. I know," he told the dog.

The answer was a resounding *yes*. To both.

Sixteen

"I've never been so tired in my life," Addison said, rocking the car seat on the chair next to her. "I'm not sure how it happened but she's completely nocturnal. Do you think Bran is secretly a vampire?"

Gia laughed. She invited Addi out of the house for lunch, knowing that Bran's wife was climbing the walls. Work was Addison's favorite pastime, which she'd swapped for staying home with her daughter during her maternity leave.

The day was sunny and beautiful so they'd opted to sit outside at the swanky café midway between their houses. Soft jazz music played in the background interspersed with the light tinkling of silverware on plates.

"At least Quinn sleeps when you're out of the house." Her niece's eyelashes cast shadows on her chubby cheeks, causing Gia to smile again. "And you know I can come over and help whenever you need me."

"I know. You're kind of awesome like that."

"Best aunt ever." Gia pressed her fingertips to her collarbone. She'd loved both her nieces on sight, couldn't get enough of them.

She and Jayson hadn't seriously discussed children when they were married. They were always waiting for work to slow down, or for things between them to settle. But now with two of the most beautiful babies on the planet in her immediate circle, she could admit she'd been thinking a lot more about the family she might have some day.

The problem was she couldn't picture a man in the role of father to her children—save one.

Guess who that was?

Now that they'd had slept together twice, she wasn't sure what she should be doing. Breaking up with him to search for Mr. Forever, who she was seriously doubting she'd find on that dating app? Or continuing with Jayson knowing that they wouldn't work permanently?

"I feel like Royce and Taylor have been on their honeymoon for a hundred years." Addison stopped rocking her daughter and ate a bite of her strawberry spinach salad.

"Right? He becomes CEO and then turns into a big slacker." Which wasn't true at all. Her oldest brother deserved a break.

"How is the tablet thing going?" Addi asked. "Have you and Jayson cracked the code?"

"Not yet. We've been working on it, though."

"Must be hard to work that closely with him and not

want to strangle each other. Or, you know, have sex in the bathroom." Addi smirked.

Gia shook her head. "Knew that was coming."

"Come on! Give me something. You have sex for the first time since your divorce and you're not going to dish even a little?" Addi tilted her head. "Wait—that *was* the first time, wasn't it?"

"That was the first time," Gia confirmed, then offered a coy smile. "Though we did do it in the car five days before the divorce."

Addi laughed, pure glee as she stabbed her salad.

"You're enjoying this."

"I really am. I haven't been out much," Addi said. "So, what else can you tell me? Now you're working together and having sex all over the house?"

Gia lifted one half of her club sandwich. "Only once. By the pool. And it wasn't a good idea. Especially after my date with Elias."

"You went on a date?" Addi gaped at her. "Who's Elias?"

"A guy I met on the app." Gia bit the corner of her sandwich. "He was…" *Not Jay.* "Nice but boring."

"Well, one thing's for sure. With you and Jayson, things are *never* boring."

Gia ate a french fry. Things between her and Jayson were never boring because they were unresolved. It was like there were arguments floating in the air between them. Things they'd never said as well as things that had been said way too much.

"I'm not sure what we're doing," Gia admitted. "Jayson and I. We've done this already—the whole shebang. Wedding. House."

"You don't have to figure that out now," Addi said practically. Quinn cooed and Addi rocked the car seat.

"No, but we'll have to figure things out eventually."

"This is where your big brain gets you into trouble. Sometimes you just have to go for it and see what happens next."

"You mean like you did with Bran." Gia folded her arms on the table and lifted one eyebrow. Addison had leaped before she looked with Bran and they'd suffered a setback because of it.

"Just like that." Addi nodded, surprising Gia with her reaction. "It worked out in the end. There's no right way to do what you're doing. And you don't have to protect yourself with Jayson. He's the safest bet you have."

Yes, in some ways he was safe. He wouldn't hurt her. He respected her. He'd give her the best time of her life in bed.

But he was also unsafe—because every time he was around her, she couldn't seem to separate the man who'd broken her heart while they were married from the man who'd won it early on.

She didn't want to dive in headfirst again only to discover they were still in the shallows. Any attempt at a long-term relationship could land them back in the same situation they were in before.

And she couldn't stomach ending things with him again. It hurt too much the first time.

The conversation with Addison looped in Gia's head when she returned to work, crashed into her when she climbed into her car to drive home, and arrived on a silver platter when Jayson showed up at her house twenty minutes later.

The front door opened and her heart zoomed to her toes. He walked in, a leather shoulder bag in his hand. "It's just me" might as well have been a "Honey, I'm home."

She was in the kitchen, the makings for a sandwich spread out on the countertop.

"No takeout tonight?" He examined the counter-top: mayo jar, bakery-fresh whole wheat bread, leaf lettuce, a freshly sliced tomato, smoked turkey breast and a jar of pickles.

"You're welcome to have one."

"Thought you'd never ask." He hesitated, his eyes lingering on her mouth. She licked her lips self-consciously, knowing she shouldn't want the casual peck hello but wanting it anyway.

In the end, his mouth flinched into a tight smile and he leaned past her to pluck a pickle slice from the jar.

As homey as this scene felt, they were still separated. She'd do well to remember that.

He set his bag down on a bar chair and rubbed his hands together. "I need chips."

"On top of the fridge," she answered automatically. But he knew where the chips were in this house. He'd been the one to store them there to begin with. Why she'd kept them there when she had to grab a footstool to reach them was beyond her.

He was right. Some things never changed.

"Before you met me you crammed them into a cabinet and broke half the chips in the bag." He sliced open the bag with a pair of scissors from a drawer he was also familiar with. The entire scene was eerily familiar. As if they'd time-traveled back to when they were married and this was a typical day after work.

And yet it was utterly and totally different.

What was it that Jayson had said the last time they'd slept together? *I don't want to fail with you again.*

He hadn't said, "I don't want to fail you" nor had he said, "I don't want to fail." He'd said, "I don't want to fail *with* you," as if they'd both had blame in what happened between them.

She couldn't remember a time when he wasn't justifying his position and his actions. When he wasn't and expecting her to go along with what he'd decided should happen. He never listened, and she never felt heard.

Had he changed in the year and a half they were apart? Or was that dangerous and hopeful thinking?

They made their sandwiches side by side in silence.

"Why did we buy such a big house?" she asked as she traversed the wide layout of the kitchen to the trashcan.

"You love this house."

"I do but it's too much—" Especially now that it was just her.

He navigated a huge bite of his stacked turkey sandwich before speaking. "You loved it and I wanted you to have it."

Both true. She'd stepped into this very kitchen and had done a twirl reminiscent of *The Sound of Music* on the marble tile. "I did love it."

"You talked about huge Christmas dinners prepared in this oven," he reminded her. "And kids running through the halls. You wanted a dog at one point. Remember?"

A dog. That's right. She remembered.

Remembering hurt.

And now she couldn't begin to picture another man—like Denver or Elias—in the kitchen eating over the counter. One who didn't smash potato chips between his sandwich before taking a bite.

"We've had some pretty late nights." She needed to tell him what she'd been thinking. Establish some boundaries for both their sakes. "If you don't want to drive home, you don't have to."

His eyebrows lifted in interest. "Oh, yeah?"

"The pool house is all yours," she said, before he had the very wrong idea of what she was offering.

No matter what fun with Jayson she could have, Gia knew what was at stake. Being with him in this familiar environment was chipping away at her resolve. She didn't need the constant reminder of what they could have had—of what they'd once naively dreamed they could have.

"The pool house," he repeated, his tone flat.

"Sure. There's a lot of unused space out there. I still have that bed out there."

He watched her, his eyes darkening to navy blue. "I know that bed, G."

She couldn't look away even though she should. She knew that bed, too. While the house was filled with decorators for nearly a month, she and Jay had stayed in the pool house. They'd made love on that small double bed, woke to a view of the pool and their backyard.

He would rise before her and make coffee in the cheap four-cup coffee maker and deliver her the first cup.

Simpler, better times.

It seemed no matter where she looked she couldn't escape memories of them together. How was she supposed to make a life on her own for herself when she couldn't leave *them* behind?

Seventeen

He'd nearly cracked the code by nightfall.

Gia had gone to bed before him, leaving him in the family room to work. He apparently now had two options. Drive home or sleep in the pool house.

It irritated him that she wanted to kick him out. They'd been close lately. Why the sudden line in the sand?

He shut down Big Ben and pulled his keys from his pocket, frowning down at them. He didn't want to go home. He wanted to stay here—and *not* in the damn pool house. He couldn't escape the idea that Gia needed him here, in the *actual* house.

Not to protect her—the gated community was safe. And the security system he'd insisted she install after he moved out was top-of-the-line. But to just…*be here*.

She'd seemed sad after telling him he could stay in the pool house, and he didn't want her to be sad and alone.

So, he laid down on the couch anyway, his arm thrown over his head, eyes on the ceiling. He slept a little and thought a lot. About the arguments they'd had behind these walls. Those once impassioned disagreements that turned into apathetic silence, which then led them to split in the first place.

Around six thirty in the morning, he heard her shuffle into the kitchen. He was already at the desk, bleary-eyed and tired, since he'd thought a lot more than he'd slept.

"Morning," he croaked, to let her know he was there.

"Morning." Her dark hair was scooped into a top-knot and she wore a short silk robe, white with big black flowers on it. She looked soft and approachable and adorable, and his hands itched to touch her.

"You're wearing glasses," he observed as he stood to stretch.

"They're new." She touched the frames. "I usually wear contacts at work."

"Oh." So much had changed, and yet whenever he was here he was somehow frozen in time.

She scooped coffee grounds into a filter basket. "Coffee?"

"Sure."

She pressed the button on the machine and propped her fist on her hip. She was cute and sleepy and damned sexy. Especially in those dark-framed glasses. "You didn't sleep in the pool house did you?"

"How did you—I didn't feel right leaving you."

He lifted a hand to his hair, feeling strangely uncomfortable.

"And you in my house when I told you to leave felt *right*?"

"What are you trying to avoid by kicking me out, G?"

He could feel the sexual tension between them right now. She was likely trying to avoid this very situation. Them, together, wearing very little.

"You never listen. I have been sleeping alone for a while now. I don't need a guard downstairs."

He opened his mouth to tell her he wasn't guarding her, he wanted to be here for her in case she needed him. But old patterns threatened. If he said that, she'd tell him that he could let go of the need to take care of her since they were divorced.

He didn't want the conversation to go that way. Time to try something new.

Vulnerability.

Hadn't that been what Chester recommended?

Jayson didn't have a good track record with vulnerability. His father had seen it as a weakness to exploit, and his mother felt guilty that she'd caused Jay to feel unsafe. He'd shored up his emotions for a damn good reason—to protect himself and the people he loved. Only now he wondered if opening up to Gia might be the what they needed to bury their past once and for all. Still, opening up could be the ultimate humiliation for him if she rejected him—totally possible.

He needed her closer for this conversation. Tucking a finger into the silky belt at her waist, he pulled her to him. "You like to remind me how much you don't need me, which makes me feel rejected."

She blinked up at him. Now that he'd admitted what he was feeling, what he was *feeling* was exposed. Might as well have loaded a gun and handed it to her. Rather than backtrack, he decided to lean in a bit more. "When we were together I went about protecting you in the wrong way."

Her eyes widened. She stared as if shocked by his words. For good reason. He'd rarely if ever admitted as his mistakes in the past. He'd always thought he knew best.

"I care about you," he said. "I never meant to hobble or limit you. I never intended for you to feel like you were a child I was looking after. Despite not wanting to be like my dad, I guess I had a heavy hand after all."

No, he'd never physically harmed her, but trying to stifle her when she should be wild and free hadn't been much better.

She reached up and placed her hand on his cheek. "No, Jayson. You're nothing like your father. I heard the stories from both you and your mom, and I believed then what I believe now."

He stayed silent, as if part of him knew how badly he needed to hear what came next.

"You're overprotective at times, but you're also kind. And sweet."

He grumbled.

She laughed and patted his cheek. "It's okay to be sweet. You're not your dad. You could never be that small of a man."

The moment called for a kiss, so he bent his head. She inclined her chin to meet him in the middle.

Maybe vulnerability had its merits.

She tasted like Gia. Like the woman he hadn't seen at this ungodly hour since he'd awoken next to her in the bed they shared. It was a bed he'd like to share with her again…say, right now.

She surprised him by reaching up and clinging to his neck, kissing him deeper. He untied her robe, slipping his palms over her warm skin. Beneath he found a simple white tank top and black panties. This outfit was one of his all-time favorites. No fancy lingerie needed, his ex-wife was sexiest when she wore cotton.

He sucked in a breath as he lifted the edge of her tank and tickled her skin. "So soft."

Her own breathing sped as her hands roamed over his T-shirt. "We have to go to work," she cautioned, but there was no conviction in her words.

"And if we don't?" He wrapped his arms around her and pulled her flush against him. He was already hard from that kiss. "When was the last time you did something you weren't supposed to, Gia?"

She laughed, the sound husky and sexy, and turned those dark eyes up to him. Her grin held. "It's been frequent since we've been hanging out more often."

He liked that.

He lifted and deposited her on the countertop, content to use the momentum they had to spend some serious quality time with her. Just as his mouth stamped hers and his hand closed over her breast, a sharp knock came from the front door.

"It's us!" Taylor Knox called out. She hadn't made it into the kitchen yet, but she would soon enough.

"Crap! I forgot." Gia shoved away from him and hopped off the counter.

"What the hell...?" He adjusted the part of himself that had recently become large enough to be a distraction.

"Royce and Taylor asked if they could swing by on the way to work today to drop off something."

"What something?" It'd better be important, that was for damn sure.

She waved him off. "Go hide."

"Hide?"

"Jayson, it's seven in the morning and neither of us are dressed."

"Last I checked we're not teenagers. You have nothing to explain." He folded his arms. He wasn't going anywhere. "You're a grown woman." As a grown woman she could sleep with Jayson—or *almost* sleep with him—anytime she liked.

"At least act casual?" she pleaded.

"Casual went out the window with that kiss."

She glared, a sure sign she agreed, and then walked out of sight.

A moment later, Taylor was chattering her way excitedly through the house. Royce's low murmur followed. Jayson poured himself a cup of coffee and leaned against the countertop. When Taylor entered the kitchen, her sentence trailed off into an ellipsis.

"Hi, Coop," she said carefully, exchanging glances with Royce before swapping a lengthier one with Gia.

"Morning." Jayson sipped his coffee.

"Cooper." Royce's expression was harder to read than his wife's.

"Coffee?" Jayson offered.

"No, thanks," Taylor said. "We brought a few souvenirs and I wanted to drop them off before Gia took off for work. We have something for you, too, but it didn't occur to me to bring it."

"For good reason," Royce murmured. "We didn't expect to find you here." He didn't often play the big, bad brother card with Jayson—or at least he hadn't in a while. If he thought he was intimidating... Hell, Jayson was older than Royce.

"Why don't we have our coffee outside," Royce added.

"I'll have mine right here, thanks, but you can go outside if you like." Jayson grinned.

Royce glowered for a beat before Taylor interrupted the short standoff.

"We should go. Don't you have to be in the office soon?" Taylor asked her husband.

"Nope."

"What's the matter, Royce? Afraid to admit your feelings in front of your sister? She's an adult, you know." Jayson informed him.

"Afraid has nothing to do with it." Royce faced his sister. "Are you being careful with him? In *every way imaginable*?"

"Royce!" Taylor shot him a peeved look.

"Gia knows what she wants," Jayson said. "She also knows what she doesn't want. She'd never allow me, or anyone, to trample her wishes. You know that better than anyone. She's damned well capable of making decisions for herself regardless of what you or I want her to do."

Royce's nostrils flared.

Gia took a step closer to Jayson and he instantly realized what he'd done. He'd spoken for her instead of giving her the space to speak for herself. Dammit, would he ever learn?

"Thank you, Jayson."

Wait. Did she just *thank him*?

"I'm not interested in your advice when it comes to Jayson," she told her brother." She winked at Taylor. "Yours I'd consider."

"Aw, thanks, G." Taylor smiled. Royce did not. She gave her husband's arm a light slap. "Oh, stop being so overbearing. Jayson's right. Gia can take care of herself." Taylor set the gift bag on the counter before curling her arms around one of Royce's. "We'll be leaving now. See you at the office."

Once they'd gone, Jayson turned to his ex-wife. "Did I have a stroke or did both you and Taylor admit that I was right?"

"Don't ruin this moment by being arrogant." But Gia was smiling when she said it. She pulled the coffee cup from his hand and set it on the counter. "Now, where were we? We have a few minutes to continue what we started before going in to work."

He didn't hesitate, setting her on the countertop next to his coffee and kissing her.

They didn't end up having sex, but second base wasn't bad.

Eighteen

The moment Gia sat down at her desk later that morning and opened her laptop Taylor appeared as if a magician had *abracadabraed* her there.

"I leave for my honeymoon and apparently miss a really big development between you and Jayson! Did you not each bring your own dates—the first time I've ever seen that happen, by the way—to my wedding? Tell me everything. Every last thing." She dragged a chair over and sat, elbows propped on the desk's surface, chin in her hands.

"Well—"

"Addison told me you had sex after the wedding, but I thought she was mistaken. I mean it was the morning after and there were still guests mingling at the breakfast bar."

"Well—"

"I never believed you with that skateboarder for a second. Or Cooper with that model." Taylor rolled her eyes. "Give me a break."

"Yeah, um… Our dates weren't really doing it for us."

"So you did it to each other?" Taylor giggled at her own joke. "Sorry about busting in on you two this morning."

"It's okay. He wasn't supposed to be there, actually. I asked him to sleep in the pool house."

"Boundaries are important," Taylor said carefully.

About that… The second Taylor and Royce left, Gia happily made out with Jayson. He'd admitted he handled things poorly when they were married and then defended Gia to her brother. It was beyond sexy hearing him say she could handle herself. She'd wanted to see that change in him for so long. Now that she had, she was having trouble trusting it.

"Sex is a normal, natural thing," Taylor said. "If that's where you and Cooper are, enjoy it."

"You, too? Addi told me to go for it. It's not that easy, you know. Jayson and I are divorced."

"Yeah, and you're still human. Plus, you two have a very unique relationship, even with a marriage behind you. Mistakes are always made in relationships. Sometimes you have to grow and learn. Maybe your timing was off the first time around."

"Or maybe I'm going to lose my heart to the one man I should know better than to hand it to." Jayson was a wonderful person and hotter than Hades in the summertime but him admitting he'd overstepped one time wasn't going to fix everything.

"Oh, honey." Taylor patted her best friend's hand. "I love you. I wish you every happiness in life, whether you end up sharing a life with Jayson or not. But sometimes you have to take a leap of faith even if you're not sure it's going to work out. Look at me. After all the mistakes I made, I have Royce. I have Emmaline. Can't blame me for wanting you to have that same happiness."

"No. I can't blame you." Gia smiled. What Taylor and Royce had was beautiful and everlasting.

"It's okay to screw up." Taylor stood. "I know you think you have to be bulletproof—to hold your own and make sure you do everything for yourself, but in the end it's not worth it. It's okay to admit you messed up. Messing up is a sign that you tried."

Gia *had* tried in her marriage, but she was haunted by the worry that she hadn't tried *enough*. If she and Jayson were to realize they'd made a mistake divorcing, would she ever be able to forgive herself for causing them so much pain? After all, she was the one who'd offered divorce as a solution.

Rather than say any of that, she nodded at her friend. "Thanks, Tay."

"You bet, doll." Taylor slipped out of Gia's office at the same time Jay passed by the door. He stopped and leaned in, both hands on the door frame. He looked good. Somehow better than he had a few hours ago. She was struck with the overwhelming need to touch him.

"Brainstorming sesh tonight at the house?" he asked. *The house.* He'd worded that carefully. "Sure."

"Wine?"

Maybe she'd been overthinking—a hobby she was intimately familiar with. Maybe she should take her sisters-in-law's advice and enjoy the moment. "Sure."

"Red? White?"

"Chardonnay would be lovely."

"Consider it done." He tapped the door frame and walked away. She watched him go, admiring his strong, straight back, dark wavy hair and long legs.

That night Gia was propped up on her sofa, tablet in her lap. Jayson sat at the desk on the other side of the room.

She thought about her conversation with Taylor when she should have been focusing on solving the tablet issue. No one on their team had made headway. When she suggested to Jayson they should scrap the update, he nearly blew his stack.

We can't let this beat us, G. Those improvements are vital to the survival of this tablet. If we give up now, we're signing its death warrant.

That made her think of them, their marriage. Had they given up rather than improve?

The longer she sat in the same room with him, the more irresistible he became. That same old familiarity smacked between them, here in their former shared house. Even when they weren't having sex, she felt the sizzle of attraction. Even with the unromantic pizza box on the coffee table, what was left of their dinner having congealed into a rock-hard mass of cheese and olives.

It was important for her to define boundaries not

only for Jay, but for herself. She shouldn't have continued kissing him this morning. She should have marched upstairs and dressed for work, and kept her cool. That lengthy physical interaction with him made it harder for her to bury those thoughts about their marriage and the mistakes that were made. In short, it'd made it harder for her to continue moving *forward*.

She was stuck. On the damn tablet issue, and on Jayson.

With a sigh, she restarted the tablet for the nine-hundredth time and began poking around. As expected, it powered down before she'd had a chance to—

"Oh my God," she muttered. While part of her mind had been turning over her current situation, the processing part had shoved two puzzle pieces together. She knew *exactly* what to do to fix this update.

Jay swiveled in his chair, barely reined-in excitement in his eyes. "That sounded promising."

She had to smile. He knew her *Eureka!* voice.

She rushed to the desk, physically moved his hand from the mouse, and clicked out of what he was working on. A few clicks and keystrokes later, she knew she had it. A zap of intuition told her that she'd tripped upon exactly the right code.

She was a superhero.

"That's it. The fix. I know it. I know it, I know it…" Heart racing, she stood over the desk staring down at Jayson, her chest rising and falling with each truncated breath.

"Why am I not surprised?" His slow blink commu-

nicated that he was proud. His approval, while dangerous to covet, was oh-so welcome.

"Hand it over. I'll update the software and we'll do
a test. We'll see if you just won the bet. Or if I have
another shot at winning it myself."

Right. The bet. She hadn't been thinking about that.
Her thoughts had narrowed to fixating on him and
finding the glitch.

What felt like years later, but was more like fif-
teen minutes, she chewed on the side of her thumb and
paced from kitchen to living room.

Finally, she heard the telltale chime of the tablet
firing up. She raced over to watch as his blunt fingers
tapped from screen to screen. He powered down and
glanced up at her, warmth in his blue eyes. While her
breath stalled in her lungs, he powered up the tablet
one more time and tapped on the screen.

"It didn't crash. *Yet.*" His lips curved. "The shut-
down typically occurs immediately. Just to make sure,
have at it." He handed over the tablet and instructed
her to test it for herself. "I'll do the same with mine."

Jayson opened one webpage and another, and then
another. He opened a social media app. He uploaded
a game, played it for a few minutes, and then closed it
and opened a documents file.

No crashing. Not a whisper that anything hadn't
been operating before.

She did it. *She did it!*

He was thrilled and awed by her brilliant mind.
He was also disappointed for not discovering the fix
himself. Had it been his stroke of genius that fixed the

tablet, they'd be naked by now, her under him, moaning his name.

Not that he was giving up.

"Anything bad happen yet?" he asked.

"Not yet." She showed him her screen. "Other than a new addiction to Candy Blaster. I'm on level thirteen already. You know what that means?"

"You can blast candy with the best of them?"

"Har-har. It *means* I am owed a homemade pasta dinner." Her grin was contagious. Once upon a time she'd called that recipe a "panty dropper."

No, he wasn't giving up on getting her into bed yet.

He rose and walked to the sofa. "You should be proud. An issue that stumped the best minds at Thom-Knox didn't stand a chance against yours."

"Thanks." She gave him a sheepish smile. He loved her humility, even though he'd argued with her to own her smarts on more than one occasion.

"I'll let everyone know the race is over, then I'll head to the office." He grabbed his tablet and bag and slung it over his shoulder.

"Now?" She stood and fidgeted with her own tablet. "I mean. We should at least soak in the win."

She didn't want him to go? Interesting.

While he would be the first to admit that a celebration was in order, he also knew she'd been hard at work on this for long enough. Once the adrenaline wore off she was going to be exhausted and grouchy. He could handle both, but he wasn't sure she could handle both with him around.

"I don't want to wait another second to input this fix in the system. Good job, Gia. Killed it." Rubbing her biceps with his palm, he leaned down to kiss her on the cheek. When he pulled back she turned her head, her dark eyes seeking his with so much want he could feel it in his bones.

He thought for a second she might kiss him. Thought that her lingering gaze might lead to more. If that was the case, he'd have a hard time making himself leave, no matter what needed to be done at work.

"Okay." She blinked, at that dash of errant lust dissipated. "You owe me dinner."

"I do," he agreed. One panty-dropper dinner, coming right up. Once upon a time he'd had his sights set on wooing her. How interesting to find himself back in that same boat now. "How's Saturday? Six o'clock?"

She nodded. "What do you want me to do?"

"Enjoy the spoils that come with winning." He headed for the door and she called out good-night. He glanced at his hand on the doorknob, all but forcing himself to leave the house and her behind tonight.

"Good night, G," he said to himself once he was outside.

Nineteen

Jayson sat on the corner of his desk in the center of the tech department, addressing his team. Everyone was sitting at their surrounding desks, eyes on him while he delivered the very good news that the software glitch had been *unglitched.*

Gia lingered at the threshold of her office, arms folded, hip propped on the doorway. In case anyone was watching her, she needed to appear both supportive and comfortable. The supportive part was easy. Jayson was amazingly adept at work and was a respected and admired leader.

The comfortable part took some doing.

Watching him sit there, one foot on the floor, the other dangling off the corner of the desk, his hands folded between the spread of his thick thighs made her want him. The way she'd wanted him last night.

He hadn't tried anything and she kept telling herself she was glad. After all she'd been trying to establish boundaries.

And now, voilà. *Boundaries*.

His team laughed at something he said and Jayson smiled. He had an easy way of wielding power. Like a gladiator in the ring who knew he was in charge of the crowd. Even the standard office attire of a gray-blue button-down shirt and dark tie, dark gray pants and leather shoes didn't distract from that power.

She had been surrounded by powerful men all her life. Men, this one included, who thought they knew what was best for her. She'd never been intimidated or afraid to stick up for herself. She'd never been afraid to speak her mind.

She recalled his moment of vulnerability, when he'd admitted he'd been heavy-handed while they were married. He had, but their problems weren't only caused by him. He'd been trying to help, which made her wonder… Had she been so concerned with asserting herself that she'd trampled on his efforts to care for her?

That was an uncomfortable thought. Almost as uncomfortable as her cheeks going warm the moment he turned his head and focused on her.

Oh, how she'd been tempted to keep him at the house a little longer. To talk him into a glass of wine and some kissing on the couch. It would have been playing with fire, she knew. So why was she so disappointed that he'd left instead?

He'd confused her lately.

She'd thought she knew him. Knew his tendency to steamroll her, and that he hadn't been the best listener, but lately she was beginning to think he'd changed. Not only had he admitted he didn't handle things best while they were married, but he'd also argued with Royce that she could handle things on her own.

She'd been unable to believe what she was hearing.

While she'd been hyperfocused on their *inability* to work things out in the past, she couldn't help thinking that fixing the unfixable tablet issue was a symbol of how much she and Jayson had grown since they'd divorced.

Her body wasn't helping matters.

Every nonsexual thing he said now grew wings and flapped low in her belly. The phrase *integrated software analysis* shouldn't make her want him.

"I appreciate the team's attention to detail," Jayson's voice dipped into an unintentionally sexy husk. "You should be proud of how hard you've worked. I know you've been sweating over the details in search of that magical sweet spot…"

As she absently twirled a few strands of her hair, her eyes feasted on the broadness of his chest. The hardness of his body. She'd stayed up past dark working up a different kind of sweat with him when they were married… And she recalled with clarity how tirelessly he'd searched for her magical sweet spot…

"Now the confession," he said, his gaze arrowing straight to her. "Gia solved the problem. We had a bet going, too. I lost."

After applause, and her demure curtsy, one of their tech gurus, Ric, called out, "What'd you lose, Coop?"

"I have to spend several hours in a hot kitchen making my grandmother's homemade pasta recipe." One eyebrow rose in an insanely sexy way. With a heated glance toward her he added, "If I would have won—"

"I would've had to cook for him," she blurted out. "Great work everyone. It was a team effort, no matter who found the glitch. Sometimes finding what doesn't work can be just as important as what does."

Jayson gave her an approving smile. "Well said, Gia." He turned back to the group. "We're going to celebrate with a party here at ThomKnox for our department. Champagne will flow, but not yet. First we have to finish the corrections that I started, coordinate our efforts with Marketing, and then put the update back on the calendar. Thanks, everyone. You know what to do."

The team turned around in their chairs, opened computers or laptops, reached for their tablets and did as Jayson asked. He stood from his desk and followed her inside her office.

"Champagne?" She asked when he shut the door. "That was nice of you."

"Nice, huh?" He took another step closer to her and she tightened her arms over her chest, refusing to let him in on the fact that her nipples were desperately trying to get his attention. "I didn't know you were going to cook for me if I won."

"Well… I couldn't tell them the truth," she whispered.

"Which was what, again?"

She ignored his devilish, tempting grin, which wasn't easy. "I have work to do too, you know."

"Yeah, yeah. So do I." Before he left, he turned. She

felt his eyes raking over her black pencil skirt and red silk button-down shirt. "Proud of you, G. I mean it."

"Thank you." She meant that, too.

His lips pulled into a quick, tight-lipped smile, and then he left the office, and left her to wonder if maybe they had both changed over the last few years after all.

After promising champagne to the staff, Jayson considered that he and Gia hadn't yet properly celebrated their win. Yes, it was a team effort, blah, blah, blah, but she deserved to toast to her accomplishments in private, and without having to put on her work face.

Outside her house, he rang the doorbell, which felt odd considering he used to live here. But as they'd established recently, they were no longer the same people who used to live here. She'd changed since then, and so had he. Now they were somewhere in the middle, and he wasn't sure if that was a good or a bad thing.

The door opened and there stood his ex-wife, in that same scintillating red shirt that hugged her breasts. She'd kicked off her shoes in favor of bare feet, which he liked even more.

"Did I black out? Is it Saturday already?" Her eyes went to the champagne bottle, tied with a gold bow— the biggest one he'd been able to find at the convenience store. "What's this?"

"It's a bow." He flicked the fringed ribbon. "I was going to go with red to match your shirt, but this one matches the label." He spun the bottle to show her a familiar gold label.

"My favorite."

"It's the same brand I chose for the party for the

team. It got me thinking that you and I never cele-brated."

She chewed on her lip, considering.

"Can I come in?"

"Only because it's my favorite champagne and I could never turn it down. Which I'm sure you knew."

"Guilty." He smiled.

"*One* glass." She stepped aside for him to come in. There was a candle lit in the kitchen, soft music play-ing from a speaker in the living room.

"Feels different in here." Like it used to, he thought, but didn't say. She had a way of putting her feminine stamp on everything. He hadn't been able to achieve this sort of warm, welcoming vibe at his apartment. It still felt stale and drab.

"I had to air out the stench of defeat." She sent him a feisty smile as she reached for the handle on a tall cabinet. "You didn't have to give me credit for fixing the glitch, by the way." Her T-shirt rode up and ex-posed her flat, tan belly.

He set the champagne aside, the bottle sweating from the ride over in the car, and placed a chilly hand on the side of her waist.

"Your hands are freezing!" she shrieked. She swat-ted him away but there was a playful glint in her eyes.

"Never could resist that move." He eased her to one side and pulled down the pair of fluted glasses.

"I could've done that," she mumbled.

"Yes, but I'm here so you didn't have to." He handed the stemware over, upside down. When she took them in her hands, she brushed his fingers. An innocent touch, but his heart mule-kicked his chest in response.

"They don't get a lot of use. That cabinet is high." That was her way of saying thank you, he guessed. Or avoiding mentioning that those were the very champagne flutes they'd toasted with at their wedding.

Had Gia been anyone else he might have been surprised that she hadn't thrown out every item that had anything to do with them, but she'd never been petty.

She rinsed out the glasses and took her time drying them while he unwrapped the foil from the neck of the bottle. When he moved to twist off the cork she stopped him with one hand.

"Wait! Don't you want to..." She gestured outside.

"Risky." He pretended to deliberate.

"Worth it," she said before dashing outside.

In the backyard, he angled the bottle so the cork would shoot into the privacy fence rather than into the sky—a mistake he'd made once before with near disastrous consequences. He twisted the cork so that it was halfway out and then popped it with his thumb. It sailed over the pool and hit the privacy fence with a soft *thump*.

"I love that noise. Smart aim," she praised. "Remember that time when you shot the cork over the fence? It must've gone a mile."

"How could I forget? It was the shot of a lifetime. If I was trying to hit Neil's lit grill, I never could have done it."

"Not for a million dollars," she agreed with a laugh. He laughed with her, enjoying the memory and the ease between them—a rarity over the last couple of years. "Guess it wasn't all bad. Our marriage."

"No. It wasn't." She took the bottle from his hand

and tilted it to her mouth, swallowing a fizzy mouthful of the very expensive champagne. He followed her lead, taking a slug from the bottle next before settling onto the chaise lounger. He patted the cushion next to him, remembering what they'd done the last time they were on this piece of furniture.

"No funny business," she warned as she sat down, proving her memory was as good as his.

"Just an innocent bottle of champagne shared between two ex-spouses. What could possibly go wrong?"

She took a drink, this time holding on to the bottle while she stared off into the distance.

He wondered if, like him, her mind returned to the last bottle of champagne they'd shared out here.

It was one of the worst nights of his life…

Twenty

Two months before the divorce

"I thought you'd be happy," Jayson growled, equal parts confused and pissed off.

Making Gia happy was a target he couldn't hit. God knew he'd tried. It made him feel like a failure when she was unhappy and lately that'd been more often than not.

"Happy?" she asked, her tone filled with accusation.

"Yes." He glugged a few inches of champagne into her glass and then into his. "You had a problem. I fixed it."

She threw her hands up. "Without talking to me!"

"What was there to talk about?"

She snatched the bottle from him, nearly knocking

over her glass. He snatched the glass before it hit the newly installed ceramic tile, sloshing champagne onto his hand in the process.

"Unbelievable," she grumbled, sliding the patio door aside and stomping outside.

With a sigh, he followed.

"You making a decision without me, on something as large as a vehicle parked in our shared garage does *not* make me happy. You should have asked my opinion."

"All you do is complain about my truck!" He'd bought the exact Mercedes she'd cooed over when they saw it advertised the other day. "You wanted something classier. You said so yourself."

"I didn't mean I wanted you to go out and buy it for me!"

"Why? Because you can buy it for yourself? I am aware of the Knox family fortune you're sitting on, Gia. You don't have to rub my nose in it."

She set the champagne bottle on the ground next to her and crossed her arms over her chest. "You're never going to understand, Jay."

He was beginning to think she was right.

"I love the car," she said. Cryptically. "But I would rather you have included me in the decision to buy it. Stop assuming you know what I want and *ask me*."

Blinded by anger, and embarrassment, he didn't hear what she was really saying. So, of course, he continued to defend himself. "All I do is cater to what you want. It'd be nice if you appreciated it once in a while."

"You want me to *thank you* for bypassing me and doing what you feel is best?"

He'd dug in then, a mistake, but he was too pissed off to change course. "That'd be a nice change of pace."

Jayson sat next to her now on the lounge, the starry sky black above them, the water in the pool still and dark.

He hadn't handled that night well. He hadn't handled much well when they were married. He constantly felt insulted. Like a failure. He'd been trying to be her hero. How was a guy like him supposed to out-hero Jack and Brannon and Royce Knox, the three giants in her life?

He couldn't.

And so, he'd attempted to prove himself over and over. But he hadn't known what she'd wanted. Finally, he thought he knew what that was.

She wanted to be heard. To be considered.

That night's argument wasn't about the Mercedes. It was about her wanting to be included in the decisions and choices in their shared marriage. He saw that now. As crystal clear as the glassware they didn't bother using.

"You're thinking about the night you bought the car," she said.

"Yes."

"So am I."

"It was the last time I saw you drink champagne from the bottle."

"It was the last time I did it." She took another swig and then handed him the bottle.

He set the champagne aside and rested his elbows on his knees, watching the water on the surface of the pool ripple in the evening breeze. "I should have talked to you before I bought it."

He sensed more than saw her shake her head. "I should've accepted it for what it was. A gift. Instead I accused you of making choices for me."

"That evening didn't go the way I wanted," he said, remembering what came next. She'd been the one to point out that if they couldn't relate on a basic level they were better off apart. He'd asked her if she cared to clarify that, and she'd said divorce wasn't out of the question.

"I told you that night I'd be better off without you." She winced.

"No, you didn't. You said we'd be better off apart. Where we couldn't hurt each other any longer. That was my opportunity to promise you I wouldn't hurt you again. Instead, I refused to back down."

He'd agreed with her. Said that if she wanted a divorce, that was fine by him. He'd been hurt, his pride bruised. His ego had taken a beating. "I thought I couldn't please you."

"In your defense, I can be difficult," she said now, but with a kind smile.

"You were being *you*. Which is exactly why I fell in love with you in the first place." He reached for her hand and intertwined their fingers. As he'd realized previously, vulnerability wasn't his strong suit—or hers. The inability for them to let their guard down with each other was probably to blame for their splitting more than anything. "It'd be so easy to lean in and kiss you."

She licked her lips and dipped her chin. Not a nod

exactly, but she leaned the slightest bit closer and peered up at him. Tenderly, he stroked her jaw with his thumb. Once he saw his future in those deep brown eyes. Now he only saw his past.

A past littered with failure and regret. A past he couldn't undo.

"But I promised no funny stuff," he murmured.

Time to stop doing what he wanted, or what he decided was right for her. Gia had gone on not one date but two in order to put distance between them. It was time for him to stop pushing so damn hard.

Pulling his hand away, he stood. She watched him, longing emanating from her like heat off the desert floor. Then she armored up.

"Drive safe." She plucked up the bottle as she stood. "Thank you for the champagne."

That's my girl.

"You're welcome."

He walked inside and she followed, abandoning the bottle in the kitchen to see him to the door. He fought the urge to turn and kiss her one last time. That would've felt too final. Like admitting he couldn't live without her.

And he could.

He'd been doing it for years.

Twenty-One

Saturday afternoon came and he showed up at the house, apron in hand. No, really. The black canvas apron read "Pasta la Vista, baby" in bold stencil print.

Gia bought it for him last Christmas. Got a big kick out of herself for being so clever. But amidst the joking and ribbing, she also went on and on about how he'd made the best homemade pasta she'd ever eaten. And that even the best local Italian place in River Grove, Garlíc, couldn't best his skills. It'd made him proud, truth be told.

He'd gone home that night and made pasta by hand, no pasta maker to be seen since he'd left that piece of equipment with Gia. He'd made enough to feed an army but hadn't taken her any of the leftovers. It seemed too personal. Too much of a throwback to the last time he'd made her pasta—on their wedding anniversary. And after they'd nearly slept together at Addison and Brannon's wedding, he hadn't wanted to risk sending the wrong message.

He found said pasta maker now, an item his ex-wife had insisted having on the gift registry, exactly where they'd put it after they moved in. Bottom cabinet on the island and all the way in the back. As he wrestled it from behind baking dishes and a large stand mixer, he wondered if she'd forgotten about it or if she kept it on purpose. If she'd been planning on learning to make pasta herself—unlikely—or if she couldn't part with the piece of machinery because it reminded her of him.

That seemed even more unlikely.

He'd ask her why she kept it, but she wasn't home. She'd told him to let himself in, that she had errands to run.

The last time she'd left him on his own, she'd gone on a date with a billionaire yacht owner. It still chapped Jayson's ass, even though he supposed it shouldn't. She was as single as he was and allowed to date whomever she chose. Lately that'd been a bitter pill to swallow.

She didn't disclose where she was going or who she was going with so those feelings of jealousy threatened to rise. He ignored them as he piled flour and dug a well, hand mixed in eggs and slowly folded that into a dough.

He was beginning to see that letting go was an art. One he hadn't mastered yet, but he hadn't been trying until now. Not really.

Over the last eighteen months he'd seen and talked to Gia almost every day. She was part of the fabric of his existence. That he no longer climbed into bed with her was a disappointment he'd managed because he had to. Then the morning after Royce's and Taylor's wedding, he'd realized something important.

Gia wanted him, too.

In the heat of the moment, they'd been caught up, time traveling back to their very first encounter, in the same damn bathroom. Which wasn't that surprising given how lackluster their wedding dates had been. But expecting to be able to continue forward without repercussions or emotions was a fool's dream.

When he'd brought the champagne over, he'd learned just how much of that baggage existed for both of them. The memories, the arguments. Sex—even really great sex *twice*—wasn't going to be the magic wand that erased their past.

He'd admitted his faults to her, but that was also too little too late. If he'd been a man who'd recognized in the moment what she needed, maybe they'd still be together.

He punched the dough, more frustrated with himself for being a dumbass than anything and decided that while he couldn't change the past, he could change the future.

Jayson and Gia weren't going to live happily-ever-after, but they could find joy together right now. Even briefly.

"Hey, Siri," he called to his phone. She answered, in an Australian accent, because why not, and he requested what he'd nicknamed his "Badass" playlist. His favorite song, and Gia's for that matter, was the theme song for *Rocky*.

The drumbeats started playing, those initial first few beats reminding him who he was and what he was capable of. He was going to move forward from here, as he was in this moment. He knew how to treat Gia and what she liked, and regardless of the future—whether they had one or not—they had this moment.

And this moment was what mattered.

After a shopping excursion that had yielded zero shopping bags, Gia walked into her foyer and into a wall of music. Jayson's singing voice was on point. She'd always admired his ability to carry a tune, her own talent having ended up somewhere between Brannon and Royce. Bran was an abysmal singer and Royce wasn't half-bad. She guessed that made her about a quarter good.

Jay must not have heard her walk in. Lingering at the mouth of the living room/kitchen area she watched as he shook his ass at the stove. A black apron was tied at his waist—the one she'd bought for him last Christmas, she'd bet.

A drum solo lifted on the air and he raised the wooden spoon in his hand and pounded the invisible drum set. Upon spinning around, presumably for a final cymbal crash, he spotted her.

"Hey." He dropped his arms, wooden spoon still in hand, steaming pot behind him on the stove. "I didn't hear you come in."

"You don't say." She allowed herself a laugh, because how charmingly taken aback was he, and stepped into the kitchen. Her senses went wild. "Oh my God, it smells incredible in here."

Looked pretty incredible too: her hunky ex-husband, forearms bared, scruff decorating his jaw, wearing that silly apron.

"Homemade sauce." He gestured to a pot on the back of the stove, lid on, and then to the pot he'd been stirring. "Pasta's almost done. Made-from-scratch garlic bread is in the oven."

"You went all out." She was touched. The last time he'd done that they were celebrating an anniversary. Their last, as it turned out.

"I lost fair and square. You didn't expect a jar of Prego sauce and a box of frozen garlic rolls, did you?"

"No. I didn't." His attention to detail was one of the main reasons she'd fallen in love with him. He didn't miss a thing. And he'd wanted to give her *everything*. When they were married, his attention felt smothering. Once he'd moved out, she thought she'd feel free. Instead she found herself struggling to befriend the man she'd vowed to love until the end of time.

Since that thought was a touch heavy for this homey scene, she decided to lighten the mood. "You know if you'd have cooked like this more often…"

"Don't say it," he warned, pointing at her with the wooden spoon before giving his pasta another swirl.

"I was going to say I'd be a lot fatter."

"That is not what you were going to say." Sliding her a glance, his mouth hitched into a half smile, he set the spoon aside. He grabbed an open bottle of red wine and the empty glass next to his half-full one, and sloshed in a few inches of wine before handing it to her. "Unless you'd rather chug it out of the bottle."

"Us being apart certainly didn't make you any funnier."

He grinned—full out—and she thought to herself that while he hadn't become funnier, he'd somehow become *sexier*. She eyed his backside as she sipped the fruity, deep-colored wine, recognizing it the moment the flavors burst onto her tongue.

"Is this—"

"One and the same. I wasn't going to, but then I remembered that whenever I made pasta we had this vintage."

The same wine they'd drunk on their anniversary, and their favorite from their trip to wine country that first Christmas they'd spent together. She hadn't had it in too long, fearing bad memories. But here they were, and the wine was delicious, her ex-husband was in her house shaking his great ass, and she didn't have any bad memories. Only good ones.

She'd been overthinking the night he'd delivered her champagne. She should have leaned in and kissed him—even if they'd ended up in bed together, it would have been better than soaking in the tub by herself, wishing he was there.

Regardless of the consequences.

It wasn't as if they'd end up *accidentally* remarried. They each knew the score. Their marriage didn't work because of their needs to guard their own space. They couldn't be together while also being apart.

She'd loved him, but that hadn't made them bulletproof. Admiration, friendship and sexual compatibility was one thing. Wedded bliss? Another altogether.

He lifted a noodle from the pot with a pair of tongs

and gingerly ate it. Nodding, he lifted his eyebrows before slurping the rest of the noodle down and Gia pressed her thighs together. *Soooo. Sexy.*

"Done," he announced with a nod.

"I'll go change."

"Why? You look great."

She supposed her dark blue skirt and red-striped tank and flats were suitable for a dinner at home, but she wanted to honor his efforts by stepping it up.

"I just want to. You're dressed up." she told him.

"Am I?" He glanced down at his charcoal gray pants and short-sleeved gray utility shirt—the one she'd always liked, with the black buttons.

"Give me five minutes."

"Okay." He held her eyes for a prolonged beat. His gaze was a touch daring, more playful than aloof, almost… tender. Open.

Shutting out thoughts about how she wished he would have been this open and irresistible when they were married, she climbed the stairs to change for her dinner date.

Twenty-Two

Jayson wished she wouldn't have changed. Seeing her in the low-cut navy blue dress that showcased her gorgeous breasts was torture. Also, *incredible*. He was gifted an eyeful whenever she bent over her plate.

Plus, she moaned while she ate.

Literally. *Moaned.*

He'd already been distracted by her bare legs and a pair of sexy high-heeled shoes. When she reentered the kitchen he'd nearly fumbled the bread basket. The moaning thing? Not helping matters.

"You should've been a chef," she proclaimed before taking a giant bite out of a wedge of toasted garlic bread. He'd mixed minced garlic and fresh herbs with butter and slathered it onto the bread before baking. The result?

"Ohhhhh, God." Her eyes slid shut and she tilted her head back.

Orgasmic. That was the result.

He adjusted his pants and drank down more wine. Maybe if he was super drunk he'd pass out and not be tempted to sleep with his ex-wife.

Again.

"If I were a chef, who would run your tech department?" Work. Talking about work wasn't sexy.

She swiped her mouth with a cloth napkin. "Duh. Me."

"Then who would run Marketing?" Fork hovering, he waited for her to answer but instead she twisted her lips to one side.

"We'd find someone." She shrugged one petite bare shoulder. A shoulder he wanted to kiss.

"Someone better than you?"

"I'd rather be in tech, anyway."

"You were. Before we split."

"You were there first," she argued.

She'd left the department—while not *physically* leaving the department. Her office was the same as it'd been back then. He'd originally given her the space since he felt as if he'd taken the job that should have been hers.

He wound pasta on his fork. "I would have thought you'd jump at the chance to be CEO when your father retired."

"I was too busy putting out marketing fires to even think about it."

He knew that. She worked hard.

"And now?" He leaned in, interested to hear her plans.

"I'm happy for Royce. And I'm relieved that the position of CEO didn't come between him and Brannon."

"What about you, G? What do you want?"

She blinked at him as if she was stunned that he'd asked. Had he ever asked her? Had anyone?

Damn. He'd been an ass.

"I want world peace." She gave him a disingenuous smile and then ate a bite of garlic bread. "What's wrong, do you want me out of your department?"

"You know I don't." He liked her there. "I need your brains."

"Finally, a man who loves me for my brains." She chuckled before going quiet. Probably because she'd mentioned the *L*-word. Love seemed to be tangled up between them and whatever they were to each other now. It was easier to compartmentalize before they'd had sex. Before he'd been sleeping over. Before he'd made her pasta and brought anniversary wine.

"I always appreciated how smart you were," he admitted. "I also appreciate how kind you are. How giving. Admit it, you wanted to kick my ass out of the tech department but you didn't want me to be exiled."

"My family never would have let that happen." A dodge for sure, but he felt justified that he was right.

"But you're doing well without me," he said.

"Without you! You won't leave!"

"You went on a date after we slept together, G. I can take a hint."

"This again?" She dropped her fork. "Elias and I didn't connect. He was as boring as plain oatmeal."

Jayson sat up taller. He liked hearing that.

"Plus you can't be mad about it since I returned home and had sex with you right away."

"You were the one who stripped down to a bikini."

"And you were powerless to stop yourself?" Her smile held and he didn't look away this time. Despite her trying to be blasé about this entire interaction, sexual tension was strung between them, power cable thick.

"I can stop myself." His voice was a low growl. "What do you think I'm doing right now?"

"What if…" She lifted and dropped one shoulder and studied her plate. "I don't want you to stop yourself? What if…" She met his gaze and batted her thick dark eyelashes. "I want to cut dinner short and take you upstairs?"

His entire body screamed *yes*, from his head to his lap. His grip on his fork tightened. He said nothing. Seemed the wisest course of action since he wasn't sure if he was being pranked.

"What if—" she stood from her chair and reached behind her to unzip her dress "—I want to have sex with you right now? On the kitchen floor." She dropped the front of her dress and exposed a strapless bra, the cups pushing her breasts up and together. That's what had been teasing him during dinner. That damn bra.

"I'd say no," he bit out.

She pushed out her bottom lip into a pout and he nearly let loose the feral grin he'd been hiding. Standing from his chair he reached her in two steps and crushed her body against his. With one hand he gripped the material of her dress and tugged it down until it was on the floor.

"Upstairs. In bed. With the lights *on*."

Excitement crowded out the worry in her eyes. "Sounds good to me."

Wasting no time, he lifted her into the cradle of his arms and carried her upstairs. With every step he ascended he stomped out the warnings in his head. They were crossing a lot of very dangerous lines. This time when she retreated, would she avoid him for good?

He didn't know.

But if this was their last time, he was going to make sure she never forgot it.

She kissed his neck when he crested the top of the stairs. Softly. Gently. Her lips on his skin caused his blood to heat.

"Which room is it again?" He smiled down at her before kissing her briefly on that beautiful mouth. So precious, his Gia.

No. Not precious. Just satisfy her needs and yours.

He'd make tonight worth it for both of them.

In the room he deposited her not-so-gracefully onto the rumpled blankets.

"Still don't make your bed?" he asked as he unbuttoned his shirt.

She sat on her knees, those luscious breasts spilling over her bra and giving him a peek of nipple. "Why bother? When I'll only mess it up again?"

She reached for his belt and while she worked at unbuckling it, he took off her bra and thumbed each of her nipples until she was squirming where she sat. She let out a moan.

"Thought you only made that sound while you ate pasta."

"Pasta and sex." She shoved his pants past his hips and he left her to kick off the remainder of his clothes.

"The two things I'm good for," he said, to let her know that he knew the score tonight. He knew she wasn't asking for a reunion. She didn't want to relive anniversaries past.

Tonight was about physical need. Sex for sex's sake.

Knee to the bed, he positioned himself over her. One side of her mouth lifted as she touched his chest and scooted herself back to accommodate him. He liked being accommodated. By this woman especially.

"Kiss me, Jayson Cooper."

"You got it, Gia Knox-Cooper." The air grew suddenly heavy. As he tasted her mouth and she wrapped her arms around his neck, he pushed out any thoughts about how she used to be his—how she still had his name. How he'd blown it over and over again and this could be yet another in a great line of mistakes he'd made with her.

Instead he focused on the tight, high breaths coming from her throat. On the feel of her fingernails tracing the lines of his back while he stroked into her. On the nip of her teeth on his earlobe.

Soon, to the crescendo of her hoarse cries in his ears, he followed her over.

And his world went blissfully black.

Unwilling to move from her spot on the bed, Gia stretched like a languid cat before curling into a ball again. Jayson had come out of the bathroom and stepped into their formerly shared walk-in closet, rummaging for what he called "those sexy gold shoes."

He was talking about a pair of Greek goddess, strappy heels she'd purchased for a Cleopatra costume one Halloween. She'd kept them, even though they were the most impractical purchase ever, because that night he requested that she wear *only* the shoes. They'd had fantastic sex, which was apparently par for course, and she'd fallen asleep wearing those shoes. She woken with strap marks crisscrossing up her legs. He'd removed her shoes and kissed every inch of her body before bringing her a very strong cup of coffee while she was still in bed.

That'd been a great morning.

He emerged with a white shoebox and shook it. "What's this?"

"I don't know. What is it?" But as he came closer and began digging through the box, she knew exactly what was in it. He lowered himself to the edge of the bed and she sat up and pulled the sheets over her naked body to peer inside.

He held up a birthday card with a dog holding a pair of false teeth in his mouth. "You kept this?"

"I like it." She snatched the card and read the inside. The inscription read "Love you, wife. J."

"The front is funny," she amended, tossing it back into the box. She stuck her hand in and came out with a refrigerator magnet from their trip to wine country that read "Let it merlot, let it merlot, let it merlot."

"I should put this on the fridge." She set it aside.

"You have a lot of random things in here." He held

up a new pair of shoe strings that were knotted together.

"They were the extra pair that came with my Sauconys. I don't have those shoes anymore."

Jayson plucked out a laminated tag. "My old ID badge from the office."

"You look like a serial killer in that photo." His hair was longer, and messy, and he had that goatee. His expression was bland and morose.

"Must have been a bad day." He held the badge next to his face and mimicked his old self. "Before. After."

"After is better." She snatched the tag and studied the slightly out-of-focus mug shot. "I liked that goatee though. Why'd you shave it?"

"I got lazy."

She scraped a fingernail along his cheek. "I like it now though. Sometimes scruffy. Sometimes smooth. You keep me guessing."

"So do you." He held her eyes for an uncomfortable beat, one that reminded her more of their past than this shoebox of paraphernalia.

"You rose through the ranks faster than anyone I'd ever seen," she said to change the subject.

"Oh yeah?" he said distractedly, pulling out her old gym pass.

"Yeah. Even Royce didn't become chief financial officer as quickly as you became chief technology officer." She'd never thought about that, actually. One minute Jayson was a web designer with talent to burn and the next running the entire technology department. It'd impressed her. She'd been so elated over his raise, she'd wanted to throw a party but he wouldn't let her.

She'd forgotten that until now.

He was frowning, sifting through the random collectibles. She took the box from his hands and set it aside, wrapping her arms around his neck.

"Guess I forgot how talented you are outside of the bedroom and kitchen."

His cocky smirk returned. "Is this your way of asking for seconds?"

"Do you mean of pasta?" She tried to sound innocent.

"I mean sex. Are you kicking me out tonight?"

She bit her lip, considering. She'd sort of forgotten about that part—the leaving part.

"I mean, whatever you want," she hedged.

"Are you asking me to stay?" He cocked his head. "Or saying I don't have to leave?"

"Is there a difference?" Her smile shook. There was a *big* difference.

"Let's discuss it at length after." He removed the sheet covering her breasts and kissed a path down to her belly.

"After what?"

"Don't play dumb with me. You and I both know you're not."

She sighed and fell back into bed, the shoebox forgotten as well as the discussion about him staying or leaving.

The next morning, she woke to find him next to her. They never had discussed it. And she tried not to think about how much she liked rolling over and bumping into his solid, warm back.

Twenty-Three

Gia had planned the pool party with her family a month ago and since she didn't have the heart to dis-invite Jayson, he was in attendance as well. Not that anyone present batted an eyelid. Her ex was part of the crew.

Only after the night he'd cooked for her, made love to her multiple times, and slept over, she was regret-ting him being there, and not because she wanted him out of her life.

She was beginning to want him back *in* and that was infinitely more dangerous.

Despite her trying not to soften around him, some-how he'd wedged into her heart.

She'd loved him when they were married, but now she loved him in a different way. What she felt for him was deep with understanding and nothing she could shrug off easily. They'd grown since their divorce, and she was fairly certain them splitting had a lot to do with that growth.

There were only so many flippant responses and sarcastic jokes she could trot out before the truth was evident to her—and everyone in her family.

She'd fallen in love with her ex-husband.

Doomed. That's what she was. *Doomed.*

How could she be brave enough to try again? After she'd failed so completely the first time? And after he'd summarily dismissed her the morning after he'd cooked for her and made love to her. He'd left, calm, cool and collected. As if he *hadn't* felt the earth shake the night before.

"I know what this was, G," he said, lingering at the front door. She had dressed in her robe and panties while he'd pulled on his trousers and shirt from last night. When she'd asked him to stay for coffee, he'd refused.

"Oh?" Her heart pounded. She was afraid to ask what he meant and afraid not to. She couldn't very well tell him she loved him, could she?

"There is a lot between us that is unforgivable. I know that a few good moments aren't enough to erase the past. Reconnecting with you was worth whatever happens next."

"Jay—"

"Hear me out. I have zero regrets on my end. I don't want you to have any on yours." He leaned down and kissed her. It felt final. Too final. "You don't have to

*find ways to avoid me, either. I won't come around
unless asked."*

Then he'd walked out the door and she hadn't seen
him until they were both at work, their office faces on.
When Bran had asked Jayson if he'd see him at the pool
party this weekend, the three of them had been standing in her office. To avoid awkwardness, Jayson had
swiftly agreed. Once Bran left, Jayson told her that he
didn't have to come, but she'd lapsed into her "no big
deal" self and told him to show up anyway.

Now he was here and splashing in the pool with her
niece and Gia feared she'd made a colossal mistake.

"Meeting in the kitchen," Taylor announced. They
were seated around the patio table, snacks in the center.
Bran and Jayson were in the water with Quinn while
Jack and Royce were enjoying a beer on the loungers.

"Girls only," Taylor added as she handed over baby
Emmaline to Royce and gestured for Addi to follow.
She nodded at Gia and then at Gia's mother. "You too,
Macy."

Gia, feeling as if there was a boulder in the pit of
her stomach, followed her sisters-in-law and mother
into the house. They stood around the kitchen island
and every pair of eyes homed in on her.

"What?" Gia asked, growing more nervous.

"Did something happen?" Taylor asked.

"Like what?"

"Like you're madly in love with Jayson?" Addison
filled in.

"Honey, it's all over your face." Macy, apparently,
hadn't missed a thing.

"Did you tell him? Did he shoot you down? Did you two break up?" Taylor asked.

"No and no. And…not really."

Taylor, unsatisfied with those answers, narrowed her eyes.

"After we—" Gia's gaze trickled over to her mom and decided to be vague "—*ate pasta*, he said he didn't expect anything from me."

"Only because you run like a startled deer each and every time he gets close," Addi said. "Sorry. I know it's not my business, and I don't want to argue with you, but I'm right."

Taylor and Macy nodded in agreement.

Unable to defend herself when she was outnumbered, Gia threw up her hands. "Fine! I love him. What am I supposed to do about it?"

"Go out there and tell him!" Taylor whisper-shouted. "We're tired of you guys skirting each other. Just lay it out there. Let 'er rip."

"How much sangria have you had?" Gia asked.

"A lot," Taylor said, "but that doesn't mean I'm wrong."

"I have so much to lose," Gia announced miserably. She could be shot down. And then her carefully constructed façade that she'd erected—the one where she pretended not to miss him and that she'd moved on with her life—would come tumbling down. Only this time she had a feeling she'd be buried beneath the rubble.

"Hell yeah you do," Taylor agreed. "But he might surprise you. We're going to leave soon. You should talk to him once we're gone."

"So are we. Quinn needs a nap and so does her

mom." Addison smiled warmly. "Go for it, Gia. If the worst happens, we'll be there for you."

"I'll corral your father out of here, too," Macy promised.

A second later, Gia was enveloped into a hug from all three women. Feeling excited, nervous and...yeah, mostly nervous, she wondered what Jayson would say. She wondered what she *wanted* him to say.

She wasn't expecting a proposal, but was it too much to hope for a reunion? Even one where they continued on the path they were on would be better than nothing. Though she was risking *nothing* as well, wasn't she?

Admitting to him that she loved him could push him away completely. He seemed so *done* the other morning when he'd pragmatically explained she didn't need to worry about him being in her space. And when Bran had asked if he'd be at the pool party, Jayson had been quick to tell her she could disinvite him.

He could revert to form and tell her how she *should* feel. But she held out hope that he'd listen to her this time around. That he'd be the man she continued to want and need.

The what-ifs were killing her. There was no way to know for sure which outcome to expect... She'd just have to confess, and hope for the best.

The next hour passed easily. Her family made no more mention of love or whether or not Gia talked to Jayson yet. As promised, Taylor and Royce filtered out, Addi and Bran right behind them.

Macy still hadn't managed to corral Gia's dad, but

everyone knew that Jack Knox was almost as hard to corral as his daughter.

"I'm not leaving until I have ice cream cake," he declared with a white-toothed smile.

"I'll get it," Jayson offered but Macy pushed him back onto the lounger.

"You keep Jack company. Gia and I will get it."

Gia found herself back in the kitchen at the same countertop, facing a similar firing squad as before, only now there was only one gunner.

"How are you? Are you losing your nerve?" Macy asked as she pulled the cake from the freezer and opened the box.

"There's a lot at stake, Mom."

"Marriage isn't easy. Whether you've tried it once or four times."

"How would you know if you're in the *once* club?" Gia pulled a knife from the drawer and began cutting the cake.

"Because husbands and wives change each decade so it feels like multiple marriages," her mom joked. "Everyone makes mistakes. Jayson has made his, you've made yours. The trick is being able to admit them and forgive each other."

"He's different," Gia said, thinking of how Jayson had behaved lately. "He talks differently. I know it's dangerous to think people change, but—"

"But they do. That means you've changed, too. Have you been honest with yourself about that? Have you showed *him* you're different?"

Gia felt the sting of tears in her nose. "Of course not. It's all his fault, remember?"

"Don't be glib with me, Gia Knox-Cooper. You have been gracious and poised about this divorce. You've also been an insufferable smart-ass."

"Mom."

"I love you, but if you don't start going after what you want in life, you'll forever accept what you're given instead. You've been trying for years to escape the shadow of your father and brothers. Now you have a chance to make your own choices, and you should choose what *you* want for a change." Her mother plated the slices of cake. "Deliver these. The sooner your father eats, the sooner we'll leave."

Before Gia picked up the plates, she hugged her mom.

Macy patted her daughter's back. "Go on."

Outside, Gia maneuvered two plates through the open sliding door. Jayson and her dad sat, their backs to her. There were having a quiet, and she guessed by the low hush of male voices a somewhat intense, conversation. She should interrupt but she was too intrigued by what Jayson was saying.

"Gia deserves it more than I do."

"It's not about *deserve*, Jayson," Jack replied. "It's about want. You want it. The same way you wanted chief technology officer."

Jayson's back stiffened. "That was a mistake."

"I promised you the tech department when you asked for my daughter's hand. You seemed excited about it then."

She blinked in surprise. Had she heard that correctly? She stayed out of sight, content to listen a little longer.

"I never should have accepted it." Jayson sounded as frustrated as he looked. "She graduated MIT with honors, Jack. She's overqualified for tech and her current marketing position."

"Hell, I know she's smart. I tell everyone that."

"Yes, you do, but you say it as if it's your accomplishment. Then you treat her as if she can't handle the world on her own. When you asked me to take care of her, I thought you were being fatherly. I didn't know you meant for her to settle for a lesser role in your company."

"You didn't take care of her, though, did you? Instead she shows up with that idiot skateboarder at a family wedding. You failed me," Jack snapped, his face going red. "Don't think I haven't forgotten it."

"I failed *her*," Jayson bit out. "Not you. Our marriage had nothing to do with *you*. And since you're retired neither does ThomKnox."

"But you are seeing each other again. That might lead to more. Vice president would be a good position for you, if that were the case."

"Our marriage ended a long time ago," Jayson announced.

Upon hearing that, Gia felt as if someone had plunged a knife into her chest.

"You can't bait me with the promise of VP," Jayson added. "You can't bait me, period."

"I should have fired you the second you divorced my baby girl," Jack growled.

Macy stepped outside, two plates in hand. "*Jack.* What is the meaning of this?"

Jack turned to face his wife, spotted his daughter and promptly pasted on a smile. "There are my girls."

Stunned, Gia was still frozen in place when Jayson turned and met her eyes.

"The ID badge," she muttered. "I thought it was odd how quickly you'd advanced to CTO."

"Because I gave it to him." Jack scowled. "No daughter of mine was going to be married to a man who couldn't provide."

"Jack!" Macy gasped.

"You underestimate her," Jayson told her father. "And so did I. But at least I had the hindsight to pull my head out of my ass."

Jack opened his mouth to retort but Macy stepped in. "Not another word. Jayson, Gia. We'll be going now. Thank you for the lovely afternoon."

"This isn't over," Jack promised Jayson. Then he turned to Gia, having the decency to look guilty. "I can explain."

"Not now, Daddy." She put up a hand and kept her eyes on her ex-husband. She had issues with both of them right now, but the one with Jayson was paramount.

Her father silently followed Macy into the house. Jayson folded his arms over his chest and waited until they heard the Knox family car leave the driveway.

"I wanted to run tech," she told him.

Jayson's mouth was a grim line. "I know."

"And my father gave to it to you like…some sort of dowry?" Gross. That's what this was. "You never told me. And you had an opportunity to do so the other night."

"I only wanted to protect and care for you. I—"

"I only wanted you to love me!" she shouted, tears rolling down her cheeks. Damn him. He hadn't changed at all.

"I tried! Do you know how hard it is to want to be everything to the woman who needs nothing from you?"

She shook her head, but he kept talking.

"You could make a career out of pushing me away."

"What about the last time we were together?" she asked. "What about you leaving and telling me where we stood? That was you pushing *me* away."

"I know your pattern. The second we get close you back away. I was giving you an out."

"You were protecting yourself!"

"Oh, really?" His expression shifted from disbelief to anger in a snap. "And what about now, when your dad offered me the vice president position on a silver platter? Was I *protecting myself*?"

No.

He wasn't.

"I don't want a pity job, Jayson." She put the cake on the table, the melting ice cream pooling onto the plates in the warm night air.

"It's not pity." Exasperated, he threw up his hands. "I'm damned if I do and damned if I don't. You don't want me to give you anything, but you don't want me to take anything for myself either. And by the way, I *did* love you. So much I was stupid with it. Can you say the same?"

Yes. And she could say that right now, in fact. Judging by everything he'd just said, though, he wouldn't want to hear it. She found herself guilty of doing what she'd accused Jayson of doing—protecting herself.

"You don't have to answer that," he said. "That's the benefit to being divorced. We don't have to answer to each other anymore."

He walked around her to the patio door but before he disappeared inside, he had more parting wisdom. "Being in the role of vice president is your destiny, Gia. You wanted to be involved with tech, marketing? The entire damn company? Here's your chance. Take the VP position and step into your role at ThomKnox. For a change, claim what you deserve."

Then he was gone.

She slumped onto the lounger, her eyes clouded with tears and her mind racing. Her emotions were battling each other. She wanted him, but was afraid to tell him. She wanted to step into a greater position at Thom-Knox, but didn't want to risk failing. She'd crowed about wanting a shot at making her own decisions and mistakes. Now she had the opportunity and she was too scared to do either.

And, possibly the most depressing of all… She'd wanted to tell Jayson that she loved him but she couldn't.

He didn't love her. Not anymore.

Chester filled a small shot glass with golden liquid and pushed it under Jayson's nose.

"I fucked up," Jayson said, his speech slurred thanks to the three tequila shots that had preceded this one. He'd come here straight from Gia's. Too pissed off to drive home and stew in his own juices, and maybe a little bit needing the comfort only Chester's empanadas could provide.

As it turned out, Jayson couldn't eat.

Ches, a bartender, had taken one look at him and asked what was wrong and Jay had spilled his guts.

"It happens to the best of us," Ches said. "Now drink."

"I don't want it." But Jay took it anyway. Drinking until he forgot what an idiot he was wasn't a great plan, but it was the only one he had. After downing the liquor that'd done a good job of making his head swim already, he lay back on the uncomfortable outdoor couch. The palm trees overhead canted at an awkward angle and his stomach flopped. He was horribly uncomfortable without a pillow—as if the cushions were built out of the same hard material as the frame. He sat up as quickly as he'd lay down, his head spinning in protest. "I hate this couch."

"So do I," Mason said, stepping outside to deliver a tray of beers in pilsner glasses. "And he paid five grand for it."

Jay sent Chester an appalled look. "Seriously?"

"Shut up. This is not about my couch." Chester moved to sit on the overpriced piece of furniture next to Jayson. "You know I adore you. But, Jay, honey, why didn't you tell her you let her dad give you that position *while* you were married?"

"Secrets like that tend to grow hair." Mason sat across from them in a chair that matched the couch, but at least he had a pillow that looked squishy.

"Tell me about it. Before I had the chance, we were talking about divorce and then... I dunno." Jay felt his mouth pull into a miserable frown. He knew why he'd procrastinated telling Gia. He didn't want her to hate him and she'd seemed to be heading there at a fast clip already. And if she hated him he couldn't live with himself. Which was where they'd ended up, even though he'd tried his damndest to prevent it. "She hates me."

"She doesn't hate you," Mason argued. "She's pissed off. There's a difference. And by the way, she has a right to be. Probably feels like she was swapped for a flock of sheep or something."

"Thanks, Mas." Jay reached for his beer. Not needing it, but wanting it.

"Don't be mean to your brother," Ches warned his husband as he patted Jayson's back. "He's going through a tough time. Jay, you can stay here tonight."

"Yeah, you can sleep on our five-thousand-dollar patio couch," Mason said with a smile.

Jay surprised himself by laughing. "Pass."

"You were supposed to move on," Mason reminded him unnecessarily. "That's why you took Natasha to the wedding, right? You weren't supposed to sleep with Gia at said wedding. And you weren't supposed to sleep with her over and over again. Especially since she didn't know her own father bribed you."

"Not helping," he grumbled at his brother. Jayson's arms felt like cement. He let them lay heavy on his legs when he leaned back on the couch that might as well have been crafted of that same cement. "I do *not* like this couch, Ches."

Like that, he lost his only ally. "You two hash it out. I'm done helping."

Once his husband was gone, Mas lifted an eyebrow in judgment.

"Like if you lost the love of your life you wouldn't do anything in the world to be close to him again? Even temporarily?" Jay gestured to the house behind him where Chester had disappeared.

Mason blinked. "I didn't realize you were still in love with her."

"It's a moot point, dontcha think?" Jayson lay on the couch anyway, his spine screaming in protest.

"I don't know. Did you tell her that?"

He let out a morose laugh. "Are you kidding?"

"No. I'm not." Mason sounded scarily serious. "If you're in love with her why not tell her?"

"Um, hello? How much have you been drinking? We've said everything we needed to say and most of that was said too many times and the wrong way." Jay took a hearty gulp from his own beer glass. "And she just found out I've been trying to control her for my own gain."

"Have you?"

"Jesus, Mason. No! But that's how she sees it. And if you know Gia—and *I* know Gia—you know that the only thing that matters on this planet is her perspective." He lifted the glass again then set it aside, an idea sparking. "I know. I could quit."

"You're not going to quit. You love ThomKnox."

He did.

"I could step down," Jayson said anyway. "Give her my position. Work in the mail room or something."

"Are you high?"

"No. Drunk." But he didn't feel all that drunk. Sure,

the earth was moving under his feet, but he couldn't say he wasn't thinking clearly.

"Tell her how you feel," his brother said. "Man up. Grow some balls."

"Weren't you just banging the don't-date-your-ex drum?"

"That was before I knew you were a goner for her. How long have you been in love with her, anyway? And how much longer are you going to let your bravado stand in the way of what you really want?"

"Jack offered me vice president."

"What?"

"He said ThomKnox is adding a VP position and I was in the running. He said that my being with Gia, and seeing through my promise to take care of her, would stack the deck in my favor."

"What an asshole."

"That's Jack." But that wasn't all Jack was. He was also eccentric and grossly friendly. He loved his family with a fierceness that was hard to understand, especially when Jayson's own father couldn't have given two shits about him. But Jack also had a way of undermining his family when he had his own plans in mind.

"You weren't seriously considering his offer, though."

"No, I wasn't." Jayson shook his head. "Gia deserves it. She deserves the best. That's not me."

"That's not you?" Mason let out a sharp laugh. "Give me a break. You know I know both of you, right?"

A frown pleated Jayson's forehead.

"You'd break your own back trying to prove yourself worthy—trying to prove you're not your asshole dad. Then when Gia doesn't need you to handle her, you sulk."

"Fuck you." Jayson was aware he was sulking now, though, which pissed him off more.

"Listen, man. You chose a strong woman. That's not a bad thing. Give her what she really, truly needs, though. Don't just try and shine in her eyes. Okay?"

What she really, truly needs.

Jayson turned that over long after Mason went inside. Long after the air grew cold and his beer was gone.

Sometime during the night he came to a conclusion about what she needed. It had nothing to do with him or what he wanted.

He was going to have to give up what he wanted more than anything.

And he'd do it. For her.

Twenty-Four

By the next afternoon, Gia couldn't stand her own company any longer. She'd spent the entire morning cleaning the house. She'd thrown out the float shaped like a giant lemon slice because it reminded her of Jayson whenever she saw it. She'd even hauled the big-ass pasta maker out from under the cabinet and put it into a box bound for Goodwill.

She'd stripped the bed and washed the sheets, before going online to order a new bed so she wouldn't have to sleep in the same bed where she'd slept *with* Jayson.

What a mess. What a big, fat, stupid mess.

Her anger had spread beyond the boundaries of her person and her house, which was how she found herself at her parents' home without an invitation.

When her mother opened the front door, Gia stormed in. "Where is he?"

"Enjoying his afternoon iced tea," Macy answered as Gia blew by. "On the balcony."

Shoulders squared, Gia rerouted to the stairs.

"Don't throw him over!" Macy called up to her.

Her father's office led out onto a wide balcony outfitted with chairs, a table and an awning. She stepped into the room, rich with red leather and brass accents. Her father's *lair*.

She'd never before pictured him in here scheming. Until recently.

The French doors were open and she found her father reading the *Wall Street Journal*, a glass of whiskey and the carafe within reach.

"Gia." He smiled. The crinkles around his eyes and his puff of white hair used to be comforting. Not today.

"You owe me an explanation." She stood over him. "And an apology."

"I had my reasons."

"I'm listening."

He gestured to the chair across from his and folded his paper. "Sit. Please?"

She did, because he said *please*. She still vibrated with anger and while she wasn't going to toss him off the balcony she thought emptying his whiskey bottle over the edge might make her feel better.

"You gave Jayson the position of CTO because you didn't think I could handle it. You completely overlooked me." She'd come here for his explanation, but she had a point to make, too.

"I wanted him to feel worthy of you," her father told

her. His legs where crossed, and he rested his folded hands on one knee. "I didn't overlook you, Gia. I know exactly what you're capable of. World domination, I imagine."

She didn't smile at his joke.

"You're a powerful woman. I couldn't be prouder of who you've become. But, honey, Jayson isn't from the same world we are."

"This is about image," she said. "You were embarrassed of him."

"No." Her father's voice was firm, unyielding. "It was about him feeling as if he belonged and not like he was limping behind the rest of you. He's a good man. I care about him. I can tell you're in love with him. Still."

She slumped in her chair. "Is it that obvious?"

"I know you're mad at me. I do. And… I'm sorry."

She lifted her eyes to her father's to see if he meant it. He looked like he did.

"I was trying to make up for my mistake. I was trying to offer him vice president so you could finally have the position you want. Then he went on about you taking VP and I started talking out of my hat. You know I don't like to be challenged."

"Pretty sure I inherited that same instinct." She gave him a wan smile.

"Jayson was right. You're the worthiest candidate for vice president. I just didn't want him to leave the company, especially since you two have been…close lately."

"You were bribing him to keep seeing me?" Ugh. That was horrible.

"Incentivizing," Jack corrected. He took her hand

in both of his. She tugged it away. "I was wrong to interfere. Then your mother told me you two were, uh, dating."

Gia winced.

"I wanted to make you happy again," he continued. "You've been unhappy. I only ever wanted you to smile."

"Well, giving my job away wasn't the best tactic. I thought he'd earned that position."

"He did. He's fantastic in that capacity. I care too much about my company to hire anyone who didn't make us shine. Honestly, Gia, I thought you'd have given your brothers a run for their money when I announced my retirement. And yet you never wanted CEO."

"No." She shook her head. She had ambitions and aspirations but running ThomKnox wasn't for her.

"And after that, I didn't think you'd want the vice president position."

"I don't know what I want." But she did. She wanted her ex-husband.

"Jayson cares for you."

"He does," she admitted. "But not in the way you were hoping. Not in the way I was hoping."

Her father hummed and released her hand. "I've made my fair share of mistakes in the past—in the recent past. I'll call him and apologize. I owe him that."

"Yes, you do."

"But don't blame him for taking the tech position back then. I practically forced him into it," Jack said. "He took it for you."

"How was taking CTO from me done *for* me?"

"I told him you didn't want it. That you'd…asked me to give it to him."

"Daddy!"

"You were compensated well and I thought you would find your way to a higher rank. I never doubted you. I was trying to make sure Cooper had a place in our family enterprise."

"And he does." Jayson was a big part of the reason ThomKnox was so successful.

"How are things between you two now?" Jack asked carefully.

She shook her head. "They didn't end well. This afternoon there's a party happening at work, so I'm sure that won't be awkward at all."

Her father stood. "This is my fault."

As tempting as it was to let her father shoulder the blame, she couldn't.

"No, you only managed to tip the already leaky boat." She stood from her chair and touched his arm. "I understand why you did what you did. It was noble, in a way. I wish you would have talked to me, though. I wish Jayson would have talked to me. It would have saved a lot of misunderstanding over the years."

"Would it?" Jack frowned.

She shrugged. "I don't know. I tend to be as stubborn as you are, Daddy."

"Stubbornness is a good quality when you want to graduate with honors." He offered a half smile.

"Not so much in marriage," she said. "Compromising, I hear, is a thing."

"Stop blaming yourself. You did what you knew how to do. You guarded your life and your choices.

I'm sorry I didn't honor your union and keep my nose out of it. I'm learning, too." He held out his arms. "Forgive me?"

"Yes." She embraced him, understanding better why he'd done what he'd done. It seemed Jack had believed in her strength after all. Even though he'd gone about showing it in a way she didn't agree with.

"Off you go to claim that VP position, then?" He held her at arm's length.

"I'll talk to the executive team about it," she said. "Taylor. Royce. Brannon." She poked him in the chest. "Not you. You're retired, remember?"

"Trying to," he admitted.

Downstairs, she found her mother in the sitting room on a gray sofa, a blush pink pillow tucked at her back. Macy's charity work often spilled over into this room from her attached office. Gia took in the spread of papers on the coffee table and smiled.

"How'd it go?" Macy asked.

"He was surprisingly open. And he apologized." She sat next to her mother. "I'm assuming you two talked."

"Your father and I might have had a long talk wherein he agreed he had no right to interfere in your marriage." Macy sipped from her teacup. "Lord knows marriage is hard enough with the two people it involves."

True story.

"Did you and Jayson talk through it?"

"We argued. He left." Gia poured herself a cup of tea.

"I'm sorry."

"I'll see him at work later today. I'm still not sure what I'll say. Daddy's calling to apologize to him."

"Good."

"What are you working on, anyway?" Gia leaned forward and lifted a sheet of paper off the pile.

"A charity for abused women. It's called Heart-Reach. They help women who are trapped in abusive marriages with children to create an exit plan. You might recognize the chairwoman's name."

Gia's eyes went to a familiar name. Julia Robinson. Aka—"Jayson's mother."

"HeartReach was where she went for support when Jayson was younger—to help her escape Jay's father. I can't imagine."

Neither could Gia. "Daddy said he wanted Jayson to feel worthy. To feel like he fit in."

"Jayson had a father who didn't honor him. Jack wanted to cheer him on."

"The way he always cheered me on." Gia had always been loved. Had always been wanted.

"You championed Jayson, too, dear. When you announced your divorce, you were adamant about us not shunning him from the family. You didn't want him to lose us. Even if you were losing him in the process." Macy patted Gia's leg. "You have a great big misguided heart, like your father."

Gia hummed, finally seeing the big picture. This argument wasn't about roles at ThomKnox or Jayson having a job she'd wanted at one point. Life was about love and what really mattered. Family.

"Remarkable how Jayson turned out nothing like

his father, isn't it?" Macy said thoughtfully as she took the flyer out of Gia's hands.

"I used to accuse him of being controlling." Gia shook her head. "He was trying to be accommodating."

"Well, he could have communicated better. Men assume they know what's best. It's our job to correct them. Frequently, it seems."

Gia smiled, then sighed as the gravity of what had happened weighed on her anew. "I don't know what to do. I love him. I don't want to lose him, and I feel like I already have."

"Being brave is hard. Speak your mind. And your heart. Leave nothing on the table."

Gia blew out a breath as she swiped fresh tears from her cheeks. "Easy for you to say."

"Yes. It is." Her mother tipped her head and swiped a stray tear from Gia's face. "Can I do anything to help?"

"You already have. It's my turn to make a few decisions involving what I want. You were right. I need to step out of Daddy's and my brothers' shadows. I've been trying, but I've been going about it the wrong way. That changes right now."

"Good girl."

Gia stood to leave and then turned back to ask, "What if…he doesn't love me back?"

"I don't know how that's possible." Her mother shook her head. "Royce, Brannon, Jack and now Jayson. The men in your life fall all over themselves to protect and care for you."

For the first time in her life, Gia thought about being cared for by the men in her life. Maybe that wasn't so bad after all.

Twenty-Five

When Jayson walked into the ThomKnox building, a cup of strong coffee in hand, he didn't go straight to his desk. Instead, he entered the elevator and pressed a button for the top floor.

The executive floor was humming as per usual. He heard the quiet purr of office landline telephones interspersed with the delicate tapping of high-end keyboards. Like in the tech department, everyone had the sleekest, newest equipment and the flattest screens. Unlike tech, the desks weren't littered with candy bar wrappers or several paper cups that used to hold coffee. It was as if everyone up here knew they were in the presence of greatness. ThomKnox royalty.

Gia belonged up here.

She'd been working closely with Jayson throughout

their marriage and after, and now he saw that for what it was. He was holding her back.

As long as he remained closely intertwined with her, she'd continue to vehemently deny herself and give him favor. He knew that was because she loved him—maybe not as a husband any longer, but she couldn't turn off her emotions like a switch.

Neither could he.

He'd fallen in love with his ex-wife, against his better judgment or any iota of common sense. He'd always loved her, even when he'd been trying to bury his feelings for the sake of saving face during their rocky divorce. But since they'd reconnected, he'd felt that love on a deeper level.

No longer was he focused on gaining ground or being right. He wanted to give her what she deserved because she deserved it. Sacrifice, and vulnerability, evidently went hand in hand.

Ultimately, no matter how much money he made, no matter what kind of luxe lifestyle he lived, he didn't belong in the same category with Royce or Bran, and especially not with Gia. He'd been fooling himself. He didn't know if today's sacrifice would make up for years of treading where he didn't belong, but it was a start.

He crossed the room and silence fell. Fingers stopped tapping on keys and interested eyeballs landed on him. He felt Taylor's burning gaze as he stepped past her office and angled straight for Royce's.

They must have heard what happened after they left the house. Gia told them, or maybe Macy. It'd saved Jayson the trouble, he supposed.

He let himself into Royce's office after a brief knock. Gia's oldest brother sat up tall at his desk, his face a mask of anger. He looked as though he had something to say, so Jayson let him.

"Gia always wanted what was best for you," Royce said. "She was brokenhearted and sad after the divorce and still she insisted that nothing change between us. I honored that."

"I know you did." The Knox family had been incredibly accommodating.

"And you repay my family's loyalty by allowing my father to concoct this ridiculous plan? When you'd already accepted the CTO seat because you married Gia. If you think I'll place you in the role of vice president—"

"I don't want to be vice president. I never should have accepted the role I have now. At the time I wanted to please your father and I thought that would help Gia see me as worthy of her."

Some of the fire went out of Royce's expression. He let out a long sigh. "She always saw you as worthy, Coop."

"Sure about that?" Jayson asked. Royce didn't answer. "I was a guy from a broken home who built websites. It was crazy to imagine myself worthy of marrying into the great and powerful Knox family."

"We never made that distinction."

"You never had to. Gia loved me and Jack validated me. You accepted their approval at face value." Jayson took a breath. "I was never going to accept a VP position. Jack was being Jack. He steers his children's lives into the direction he believes is right. He was orchestrating a Jayson-and-Gia reunion."

Jack had called early this morning. He'd apologized for the things he'd said at the party. Jayson told his ex-father-in-law that he wouldn't have to worry any longer. Jayson had a way to fix everything that had happened. To set things right again.

"And now?" Royce asked.

"Now what?"

"You and Gia have been…" Royce closed his eyes as if he couldn't bear saying it aloud. "Spending time together."

"Not anymore." Admitting that aloud hurt worse than he could have imagined.

"Was it only physical for you?" Royce shifted in his chair like he was uncomfortable asking.

"Why else?" Jayson lied. He'd been close. So damn close. Before Gia had overheard that conversation and learned the secret he'd been keeping—before he'd blown everything, he'd been planning on telling her exactly how he felt about her.

That he loved her. He'd fallen in love with her again, only this time he believed himself incapable of screwing up. He'd committed to honoring her needs—her actual needs—and meeting them.

Then his past had bitten him in the ass and he realized he wasn't incapable of screwing up. He *was* a screw-up. No amount of time could fix that.

"Are you coming to the party this afternoon?" Jayson asked. "It's in celebration of the tablet fix. Gia singlehandedly saving your company and all."

"I'm planning on it."

"Good. I have an important announcement to make."

"I look forward to it," Royce said with a curt nod. Jayson couldn't tell if the other man was lying or not.

Gia arrived at the start of the party, only to bump into the party planner on her way in. "Looks fantastic in here, Joanna."

"Thank you. Everything is in place, Ms. Knox."

Gia didn't correct her by saying that her name was *Knox-Cooper*. She was too tender after everything that had happened to go there. "Wonderful. Thank you."

"You're welcome. My staff and I will be in the background making sure everything runs smoothly." Joanna, her hair pulled back in a smart tight ponytail, turned to straighten the platters of catered sushi.

Music was playing in the background and Gia walked to a bucket of ice to grab a soda for herself. Taylor and Addison were there, smiles bright.

"We're here for you no matter what happens." Taylor offered. "I'm really excited for you."

"Thank you." Gia hugged Taylor and then Addi. "I appreciate your both showing up."

"And miss the action?" Addi asked as she straightened from the hug. "Never."

"Photo booth, ladies!" The photographer interrupted.

"Not me, thanks." Gia waved them off. "You two go ahead."

The photographer shooed Taylor and Addison over to the booth and handed them each masks on sticks. Taylor, halfway to the booth mouthed the words "you owe me."

Gia wiggled her fingers in a wave, relieved at having avoided the embarrassing photo booth.

"If I could have your attention." The low sound of her ex-husband's voice came from the front of the room.

Jayson, dressed in black trousers and a slate-gray shirt, climbed onto a sturdy chair. Not that he needed to. His presence was so commanding he didn't need the chair to establish that he was in charge. His power was as undeniable as her admiration of it. She'd spent years guarding herself from that power, but now she saw the truth. That was simply *Jayson*.

"Not that anyone asked for a speech, but I have one." His eyes flicked to the back of the room and Gia turned to see her brothers enter. Bran gave her a wave, his mouth flinching into a half smile. Royce wore a frown as usual, but when he walked by, he briefly cupped her neck in a supportive gesture.

"I've been a part of ThomKnox for going on seven years," Jayson continued. "I was named chief technology officer almost five years ago, the same year I married one Miss Gia Knox-Cooper."

Smiles around the room were soft, careful. More than a few heads swiveled in her direction.

"Our marriage did not outlast the role, and I've been telling myself for nearly two years that I was okay with that. That relationships work but sometimes they don't, and Gia and I fell into that latter category. It was a lie I've been content with until recently, when I realized that not only was I in love with Gia when we were married, I have been for the entire time we were divorced."

Those soft smiles melted into gasps, Gia's own gasp among them.

"Gia is a gracious, beautiful, incredibly lovable woman," Jay went on. "She's giving. She's tough. She's strong. She's a certified genius mastermind." Nods of support came from several of their coworkers. "She's been in the role of running Marketing, and I know she loves this company with her whole heart, but Marketing isn't where she belongs. She's an MIT grad with a nerdy brain in that gorgeous noggin of hers. She loves code more than any one person has a right to. She found the glitch we're all celebrating." He cleared his throat and added, "Not me. She doesn't need me."

Her chest tightened as those words. That wasn't true. She *did* need him. More than he knew. She thought about her family members who had tried to take care of her over the years. Not because they thought she was incapable or weak, but because they loved her so very much. She'd recently learned that it was okay to lean on others; that it would have been okay to lean on Jayson while they were married.

Needing someone didn't make her unworthy. It made her *human*. Beautifully human, flaws and all.

"And yet I'm the one who's chief technology officer of this company. Or well, I was," Jayson finished. "*Was* CTO."

"No," Gia whispered. She'd made a decision about what she wanted after talking with her mother. She finally knew her goals and dreams and wasn't afraid to claim them. Jayson in the role of CTO was the *right* place for him to be. It had been all along. Her father, while he'd fumbled, wasn't wrong about that promotion.

"I love this department. I love ThomKnox as a whole," Jayson was saying. "I love Royce and Taylor, Brannon and Addison, and Jack and Macy like they're my own family." He then locked his gaze on Gia's. "I love my ex-wife enough that I refuse to stand in the way of her living the life she should be living. I should have done this years ago, G," he said, his eyes on her. "I never should have taken the position that was destined to be yours. I should have walked out the door and not looked back when you said you wanted the divorce. I should have left you at ThomKnox with your family to claim what was rightfully yours. No matter how badly I wanted to be in your orbit."

Oh, Jayson.

"I'm leaving ThomKnox, effective immediately," he said as the room erupted in excited chatter. "Gia will take over where I left off, and your upper management is more than capable of filling in the gaps. If there are any."

He stepped off the chair and that chatter grew louder. Panic laced through her stomach until she realized that she could take her power back rather than stand idly by.

"Jayson Cooper!" she shouted. No way would she allow him to make this huge of a mistake.

"My mind is made up, Gia," he said as he walked for the exit.

"And what makes you think you have the final say?" she asked his back.

He turned. Slowly. His face was a beautiful shadow of confusion and hope. She loved his face. She loved *him*.

The room grew eerily quiet. She felt every eyeball snap to her as she closed the gap between her and Jayson, her arms folded at her chest.

"As the newly named vice president of this company," she told him, her voice firm. "I don't accept your resignation."

Twenty-Six

Earlier today

"Thank you all for coming." Gia stood at the head of the conference table and addressed the upper management team of ThomKnox. "I have a proposition for you."

Brannon, tapping a pencil, eraser side down, on the table, shot her an easy wink. Royce, on Gia's left, wore a muted smile. Taylor was grinning like she'd gleaned what was coming next.

"We've been in discussion about adding a vice president position for a while now," Gia began. "And then at the pool party, Daddy decided to offer that position to Jayson."

Brannon frowned. Taylor mimicked his expression. Royce curled his lip.

"Jayson didn't accept it."

"But he had no problem claiming chief technology officer for himself," Royce grumbled.

She blinked. Royce knew plenty.

"Daddy called you."

"He called me, too," Brannon said. "We each received a Jack Knox speech about how he's failed and won't fail us again."

"He does love his grandstanding." Gia shook her head, but smiled to herself. "Jayson would make an excellent vice president. But I'd make a better one."

Taylor elbowed her husband and then bounced in her seat. "I knew it. You owe me twenty bucks."

Royce's smile came out of hiding. "I don't need twenty bucks, but we can negotiate terms later."

"Anyway," Gia said with an eye roll in the direction of her besotted oldest brother, "I want to earn the position of VP on my merits, not based on what Jack or anyone else says. I want this position. I want it to include Marketing and Tech, and then I can oversee both my passions. *And* I want Jayson to stay exactly where he is—in charge of the department he built."

"I had a meeting with the CEO, COO and president of this company this morning," she told Jayson now, aware of many onlookers, said CEO, COO and president included. "I specified that while I'll be overseeing both Marketing and Technology, I would only do it if you were involved. I need you exactly where you are."

"You don't need me, Gia. You never did."

"ThomKnox needs you." She reached down, way down, and found her bravery. Jayson had been brave enough to stand in front of everyone and tell her how he felt. She knew she could do the same. "And *I* need you," she added on a broken voice.

"Gia—"

"I never had the courage to admit that. I never wanted to appear weak in our family of titans." She glanced over at Royce and then Brannon, who each wore compressed smiles of pride. She turned back to Jayson. "Marriage is about admitting you need someone else. It's about being someone's other half."

The lines on Jayson's forehead softened as he tilted her chin gently. "I'm leaving so that you don't feel compelled to take care of me. I'm supposed to be taking care of you."

"I guess we're just going to have to take care of each other." She shrugged, vulnerable and unsure. "I mean, if that's what you want. I don't want you to feel like I'm controlling you."

A slow grin spread his mouth. "How ironic."

She grinned back at him.

"I love you, Gia. I've made so many mistakes. I've been holding on to you without realizing it."

"We both made mistakes." She gently touched his hand, still cradling her face. "And hey, I've been holding on, too. Have you checked my last name lately?"

"You never dropped the Cooper."

"I couldn't let go. Not all the way. Letting go's not the answer and you know it. We screwed up, Jay."

"Yeah. We did."

"I have a better idea of how you can make it up

to me and it doesn't involve you leaving ThomKnox. You can't leave me in a lurch and force me to find a good executive to run this department with no notice at all." She affected a stern expression. "Do we understand each other?"

"Yes, boss."

She quirked her lips. "I like that."

He leaned in to whisper into her ear, his voice a low rasp, "Only here. In the bedroom you know who's in charge."

When he pulled away, she felt her cheeks grow bright pink. "Jay," she whispered. "We have an audience."

"Right." He winked. "We'll talk about that later."

Taylor broke the silence. "To our CTO and new vice president!" She held up her plastic cup.

Addison cranked up the music.

The crowd cheered.

By the time the dancing started and everyone had dispersed, Gia and Jayson still hadn't moved from where they stood in front of each other.

"What are you doing tonight?" he asked.

"Oh, the usual." She shrugged. "Making dinner. Having a glass of wine with my laptop. Meeting the installers who are delivering the new bed."

"You ordered a new bed?"

"Yeah. I thought I wanted a different one since that other one was ours."

"And now?"

She tipped her head. "Now I'm thinking we should break in the new one. It'd be a crime to let a brand-new bed go to waste."

"Hell yes it would." He stepped closer and muttered, "Kiss me, Gia."

"No. *You* kiss *me*."

His smirk was one for the books. "Meet me half-way?"

"From here on out."

Epilogue

Laptop aglow in front of her, Gia was curled into the corner of the sofa, her eyes heavy. She just wanted to finish this one last part…

In a flash, the screen vanished, swept up by Jayson, who swapped the laptop for a glass of wine.

"I was busy!" she argued, but took the proffered glass before she ended up wearing it.

"You're always busy. You'd work until your eyeballs rolled out of your head if I let you."

"That's a charming mental picture."

"Can this wait?" He held up the laptop. Then he glanced at the screen. "Candy Blaster?"

"It's strangely addicting."

He sat next to her, his hand wrapped around her

waist. "You, Gia Knox-Cooper, are strangely addicting."

She accepted his kiss, her eyes sinking closed. Since she'd taken the vice president position, she'd moved her office from the tech department to the executive floor. Jayson took her former office and she was glad that he finally had his own space.

He was a man in charge, an executive as much as she was, and he deserved more than open office seating.

He'd been sure to remind her that *she* deserved to be at the top of her namesake company. She was a Knox and thereby "royalty" and, he'd also mentioned, again, that vice president was her destiny.

She was beginning to accept he was right. She'd done a lot of sidestepping over the years around taking what she wanted. For all her fighting for her own independence, she'd had a hard time accepting it.

As vice president she could make her mark at the company she loved. Plus, she worked closely with Taylor and her brothers, and Jayson, and that was the best part.

"I was going to ask you about that new—"

He pressed a finger to her lips and shook his head.

"Unless you were going to finish that sentence with the words *sexual position*, I'm not interested."

"Jayson!" She giggled when his fingers tickled her bare skin under her shirt.

"All work and no play, G. Don't you want a break?"

She set the wineglass aside and wrapped her arms around his neck, kissing him rather than answering. He was a lot more fun to kiss than he was to spar with, even though they were both really good at that, too.

He'd moved out of his apartment and back into the house they'd once shared. They had enjoyed plenty of sunbathing in the heated in-ground pool, and they were enjoying their new *and* old beds. Though the new bed had been relegated to a guest room. They preferred their former marriage bed for their room.

"I have a toast." He slipped away from her and grabbed his own glass.

"Now? That was just getting good." She pouted.

"I know but I have something to say. It's your favorite Chardonnay."

The crisp white Chardonnay was hard to turn down. It was her favorite autumn wine. She reached for her glass.

"To our anniversary," he said, clanging his glass with hers.

"Today isn't our anniversary."

"Not our wedding anniversary. The anniversary of the first time I saw you."

"That was New Year's Eve."

"I don't mean then, either. I'm talking about when I first saw you at ThomKnox. I was addressing my staff and stopped midsentence when you walked by. Stevens called me on it, gave me shit for a week about how I couldn't keep my tongue in my mouth."

"No! I've never heard this story before."

He set his glass aside and dropped to his knees in front of her. "Marry me, Gia." He took her free hand— her left hand. "Again."

"Why? I already have your name. You already live in my house."

"Our house."

She barely held back her smile. Her heart lifted, her mind whirred. She wanted to marry him again.

He'd learned he didn't have to prove his worth to her. She'd learned that him taking care of her was how he showed love. Being gracious was her challenge, while his was realizing he could let his guard down.

Nothing would come between them again. She knew it in her soul.

They had already agreed to communicate better, to stop trying to guess what the other one wanted, and ask instead. They understood how to give and take in equal measures. No one had to carve out their own corner. They met in the middle. Always.

"I need a new pasta maker since you threw the old one out. Figured we could register for one." He gave her a half smile.

"I do love your homemade pasta. Can we break tradition and have you make it for Christmas?"

"Gia, I asked you a question."

"I know. I'm thinking!"

"You have to think?"

"Not about the yes I'm going to give you. About which anniversary we'll celebrate in the future. Our old anniversary or our new one? Can we celebrate both?"

Grinning, probably because she'd sneaked her *yes* in those sentences, he said, "We'll celebrate today. The day we decided to make forever official. The day we decided that nothing matters more in this world than each other. The day we went in one hundred-one hundred."

"Because fifty-fifty is for losers," she whispered.

"Exactly." He rested his elbows on the couch cushions and pressed his big body against hers. Heat engulfed her whenever he was near and he was promising never to be far again. "The rings, the license, the ceremony are details. I don't care how it happens, so long as it does. Let's make a real go of it this time, G."

She put her hand into his hair and looked into his earnest, blue eyes. She was grateful, so grateful to have this time with him—to have this chance again. "I love you, Jay."

"I love you, gorgeous. Always and forever."

"Always and forever is a big commitment."

"You think of something bigger than that, you let me know." He kissed her softly and then reached into his pocket to pull out her original engagement ring… only the stone was a hell of a lot bigger than it was the first time around.

She pretended to shield her eyes from the glare.

"I won't do anything with you halfway—not ever again." He slid the band onto her left ring finger.

"How did you—"

"Your jewelry box isn't that vast," he answered. "I stole it and took it to the jeweler for the upgrade."

She admired the chunk of diamond on her finger, glittering in the lamplight. "It's *massive*."

"It's the biggest I could buy without you needing a stroller to push it around in." She laughed and he continued, "Though I'm not opposed to a stroller for you to push something else around in."

"You mean like a toy dog?"

Jayson didn't balk. "Dog. Baby. Your collection of Funko Pop! character dolls. Whatever you want, *wife*."

She put her hand on his cheek and touched his nose

with hers. "I like the sound of that, *husband*. I'm willing to give you what you want, too. That's how much I love you."

"Honey," he said in that low, growly sexy way of his, "You've already given me everything I want. Anything else from here on is the cherry on top."

* * * * *

*Don't miss any of the Kiss and Tell series
from Jessica Lemmon!*

His Forbidden Kiss
One Wild Kiss
One Last Kiss